WHEN HELL FREEZES OVER

Wicked Crown Book 2

MAY SAGE

ERIN BEDFORD

When Hell Freezes Over
Wicked Crown Book 2
May Sage & Erin Bedford © 2021
Edited by Theresa Schultz
Cover by Sylvia Frost of The Book Brander
Boutique

Lily

Most of the time, when people said "go to hell," they didn't mean it quite as literally as Roth. But then again, Roth was a demon, so perhaps the statistics didn't apply to him.

Lily hit the hard dirt with a painful thump. "Dammit!"

By luck, she had the foresight to keep her mouth shut, or she'd have been eating her first taste of the underworld right then and there. Face down on the ground, she grunted.

When she lifted her head, a small gasp slipped out of her lips.

She might have picked a bed of dirt for her landing, but the rest of Hell was spectacular. She wouldn't have had the imagination to dream it. As far as the eye could see there were opulent hills of greens so bright they could emeralds dim. There were fields of flowers in every color of the rainbow, and even some Lily had never seen before. A long cobblestone path was the only object that broke up the landscape, and even that didn't take away from the vision before her. If *this* was Hell, Lily wasn't sure going to Utopia was even worth the bother.

Movement next to her interrupted her gawking.

"Graceful." Ash snorted, easily descending beside her.

Roth had already appeared at her side. The prince of Hell had the good sense not to comment on Lily's less-than-spectacular landing.

A pair of loafers appeared before her as Lily pushed back up from the ground. She lifted her head to see Roth's hand waiting for her. With a small smile, Lily slid her hand into his, a thrill running through her from just the touch of his warm skin. Rising up, Lily found herself unable to tear her eyes away from the man before her.

The man she had dreamed of all her life was real and standing before her right now. Part of her still didn't believe it. His amber eyes bore into her, his tantalizing lips tilting up on one side as he stared right back. Lily's fingers ached to trace the line of his jaw, to feel the scruff of his beard beneath her fingers. Or on other parts of her.

She shivered at the thought.

"Cold?" Roth arched a perfect brow.

Biting down on her lip, Lily shook her head.

Roth's eyes darkened as he closed the distance, entering her personal space like he belonged there. Desire crackled between them, a living, breathing entity neither of them could deny. Roth might have concerns about them being together given their age difference, but he didn't seem to have it any easier than her when it came to wanting to touch, and feel, and *take*.

For all that, he still wanted a platonic relationship. With kissing—whatever that meant.

Right now, she wouldn't have minded a bit of kissing, though. He'd said he wasn't against it in public. They were outside, and Ash was here as a chaperon. Surely, that counted as a public setting. She could wrap her hand around his neck and—

A throat cleared. "All right, that's enough of that," Ash interrupted, stepping up next to them. "You can eye-fuck each other later. I want to know what we're going to do about Raven."

The reminder of Raven's capture was a bucket of cold water on Lily's libido.

Releasing Roth's hand, she took a step back from him. Space made it a little easier to think.

Taking a deep breath, she wrapped her arms around her waist as she thought. What could they do about Raven? She had no idea. This world wasn't something she was familiar with. A few weeks ago, the only things that had mattered to her were her exams, and managing to fly under the radar in the human world. She might have been a witch—as far as she knew—but angels and demons were beyond her comprehension and beyond her grasp.

The angels had no doubt taken her back with them to wherever it was they were hiding out. It could be Utopia or a freaking Starbucks, for all she knew. She felt clueless, powerless, and small.

"Where would they take her?" Lily looked between the two men. They were likely to know a hell of a lot more than she did about the angels' whereabouts. "They wouldn't... hurt her, would they?"

Roth skimmed his hand over his jaw and shook his head. "There's no way to know for sure. It depends on what they suspect, and also on their agenda is."

Ash scoffed. "We know what their agenda is. They want to kill her." He jerked a hand in Lily's direction. "And you know as well as I do, they have no qualms about torturing and disposing of anyone who gets in their way."

Anger billowed up in her at Ash's words. "Don't blame this all on me. I was perfectly fine before I met you." Lily felt a jolt of power travel the length of her arm and hand as she poked Ash in the chest with her finger. She'd only meant to drive her point across, but some magic pushed him back.

Stunned as she was to have called to her power without meaning to, petty satisfaction came over her when he winced.

Rubbing his chest, Ash glared down at her. "I'm sorry to burst your little bubble, princess, but this was all in play long before you ever met me. It was just a matter of who would find you first. Be glad it was me."

Lily opened her mouth to bite back, but before a word crossed her lips, she realized one annoying fact. He was *right*.

Lily breathed out a long hard sigh. "I'm sorry." The words felt like acid; she wasn't happy about the situation, but it could have been a hell of a lot worse for her. "I *am* grateful to be alive and not in their hands. Thank you, Ash."

She held back a shudder. No amount of money in the world would make her want to be at the mercy of the angels—at least not any of the ones she'd met.

Excluding Raven, of course. Maybe she didn't quite count; she was a Nephilim, a half angel, and therefore only half a psychotic asshole.

Roth stepped in and placed a hand on each of their shoulders. "We're all worried about Raven, but this isn't the time to fight amongst ourselves."

Lily and Ash nodded in agreement.

"Ash, you are the best tracker, so see what tracks you can find back at Raven's apartment. I'll send more sentinels, but you know her scent. You're the best chance we have at getting to her promptly." Roth tightened his grip on Ash's shoulder as he tried to leave. "Be careful. We don't want you captured as well. They *may* hurt Raven, but she's still one of them and Michael's daughter. You, they'd have no such reservations about."

"I don't matter." Ash shook his head. "We just need to free Raven."

"You *do* matter," Lily interjected, frowning. She couldn't believe he'd even think that. "You're my friend, just like Raven."

From the very beginning, she'd been drawn to Ash, although a certain level of fear and mistrust had tainted their relationship.

"If they get to you, we'll have to hunt you down, too, which means spending less resources on Raven," Roth pointed out.

Ash jerked his head once up and down. "Understood."

"Take care," Lily called after him. Ash had already turned his back on them and simply held a hand up in response.

"Now," Roth sighed, turning to her. "In the meantime, we must get you ready."

"Ready?" Lily lifted a brow. "Ready for what?"

"War."

Roth

They walked in silence, the implications of the last few days, the last few hours, still fresh.

"Is all of Hell like this?" Lily asked. "It's beautiful."

He could see what she was doing; she was trying to distract herself from everything going on.

Unable to help himself, Roth slipped his hand into Lily's, enjoying the feeling of her small hand in his. "We're only in the outer kingdom, Purgatory. Some places are a bit rougher around the edges." He grimaced to himself. That was putting it mildly. Purgatory definitely gave an interesting impression to those who had just arrived in Hell.

"Where do you live?" She blinked up

at him from beneath her lashes, a coy curve to her lips.

Lifting her hand, Roth pressed his lips to the smooth surface of her skin. "Why, at the center of Hell. As do you."

Her brows lifted in surprise. "Me?"

Smiling at her confusion, Roth pulled her arm into the nook of his elbow. "Your father's palace is yours by birthright. You didn't think the King of Hell lived with the lowly demons, did you?"

He continued leading her down the pathway, enjoying her rapture at everything they passed along the way; she gasped in delight, eyes full of wonder.

The noises made it all the harder to keep to his promise to stay away from her. Roth couldn't help but imagine those little sounds coming from her for another reason entirely.

"We aren't going to walk the whole way there, are we?" Lily groaned after a few moments of taking in the sights. "Not that I'm not having a good time, but if I'm going to be walking to the center of the nine circles of Hell, then—"

"Seven. And they're kingdoms."

Lily stared up at me. "Seven? What happened to eight and nine?"

"Do not believe everything you read." Roth's lips turned up as he brushed a bit of her auburn hair behind her ear. Hopefully, she would choose to go back to her natural color now that they were in Hell. "Hell is made up of seven kingdoms. Each kingdom, while laid out in a circular structure, is not analogous to the circles of Hell. We don't go around torturing sinful humans." He raised a brow at her, causing a delightful blush to cross her cheeks. Curious to know what she was thinking but unwilling to be deterred from their path, Roth pushed them along.

"We are in one of the outer rings." His free arm swept to encompass the fields. "There isn't much life here, or in many of the kingdoms; not anymore."

Lily stopped. "Why not?" Her gaze went to the fields around them, the confusion and wonder in her face ever present.

Roth could read the questions on her face as easily as if she had said them aloud. Saving her the trouble, he bent down and plucked a flower from the ground. It was purple, almost the exact shade of her natural hair color. Handing it to her, Roth peered into her eyes. "Not every demon or fallen angel wants to stay here. While it is beautiful in some ways, it can get awfully boring after a while."

"Why?"

Chuckling slightly, he tipped her chin up and gave her a quick, chaste kiss. "Eternity can become boring and..." Roth sighed, turning them back onto the path. "Lonely."

"So, you mean since you're immortal, looking at the same thing over and over every day would drive you crazy, and so everyone decided to jump ship for more interesting worlds."

"Indeed." They came to the edge of the field, where the next kingdom began. This one was less pleasant and more evocative of the realms of Dante's *Inferno*. Hardened black magma covered the ground around miniature volcano-like structures that littered the area. Heat and steam filled the air, making it almost too hot to breathe.

Roth stepped forward, but Lily pulled up short, refusing to go ahead. "What is it?" He saw the apprehension on her face, and his gaze softened. "I won't let you burn. I promise."

Lily's eyes stayed on the blazing red magma leaking from the tops of the smaller volcanoes as she allowed Roth to lead her between them.

This woman. She didn't even flinch at a hellhound, yet she hesitated at volcanos. She was remarkable in every way but was still so young. So inexperienced. Roth held back a sigh. Torturing himself with these musings wouldn't get him anywhere.

"You never answered my question."

Lily tugged on his hand as they side-stepped a sudden thickening stream of liquid magma.

He paused for a moment and then opened his mouth. "Ah, you mean are we going to walk the whole way there."

"Not that I'm not enjoying looking at my father's kingdom."

"Your kingdom," Roth reminded her. "Or it will be, once you're ready."

"And when will that be?" A nearby volcano burped, causing Lily to squeal and jump into his arms. "Can we like, skip this one? Flowers I'm good with. However, I like my eyebrows where they are, thank you very much."

Roth smirked and wrapped his arms around her waist. "Hold on." With barely a thought, his wings sprouted from his shoulders, the black-feathered limbs wrapping around them before Roth shifted and they were airborne.

Lily grabbed at his neck, pressing herself closer to him as they moved through the air and over the world below.

"Are those... hellhounds?" Lily commented after a moment, her eyes down on the ground below them. The beasts ran across the scorched ground, sidestepping the lava and small bursts of fire.

"Yes."

She held him tighter while she leaned away to see. "Is that where Ash lives?"

"Yes." Roth's jaw tensed. "Not everyone in Hell has the same comforts we do. Fights for territory are common. Now you can see why he preferred to come to Earth with me."

Lily snorted. "That's an understatement. There's nowhere to put a bed, let alone get a caffeine fix."

She tried to make a joke of it to hide the sadness in her voice. It didn't work on him. She felt the same way Roth did about their friend's life.

The way some of the lower-ranked beings were treated wasn't fair in any sense of the word. Roth was part of the haves, and Ash had always been part of the have nots. And it wasn't just Ash that hoped Lily's return would change things for the better. There was a lot of hope riding on this one petite young woman. Roth prayed she could handle the weight of it.

Ash

Being back on Earth so soon after leaving and without Raven had not been Ash's plan. While the humans treated him far better than his own, Ash just didn't feel quite at home here.

Sure, there were plenty of things here that Hell didn't have. There were movies and shopping malls. Street carts of mystery meats and five-dollar coffees. There were also bad things about Earth.

"Ash!" a high-pitched voice called out behind him on the sidewalk.

Like that.

Ash wanted to keep walking and hope that whoever it was would just go away, but no such luck. A small hand latched on to his arm and almost dragged him over.

"Hey silly, didn't you hear me calling

you?" the girlish voice grated on his nerves and made him wince.

Glancing down at the human girl Ash vaguely recognized from the college, he shook his head. "No, sorry. I didn't. What's up... Brittany?" Was that her name? All these human girls were the same and it was hard to tell them apart sometimes. They all smelled of over-priced perfumes and soaps. Not like his mate. Not like Raven.

"Bethany," she corrected, not upset that he hadn't remembered her name. She tossed her blonde hair over her shoulder and giggled again. "Where have you been? I've missed you at school."

"Oh." Ash shrugged. "I dropped out."

Bethany gasped. "Well, that's okay. I've thought about it myself. Take a year off, see the world. It would be romantic to backpack across Europe, don't you think?"

"Uh... sure," Ash answered with no enthusiasm whatsoever. He was almost to Raven's place and he didn't want this leech latched on to him.

"I'm glad you stayed around. I never got a chance to spend any quality time alone with you." Bethany stroked her fingers up and down his arm, pulling him to a stop. She fluttered her lashes in a way Ash assumed was supposed to be flirtatious. "You know, I don't have class right now. We could go back to my place and... hang out."

Ash held back another grimace at her blatant availability. "Look, Bethany, I can't. I'm involved with someone. And frankly, I don't have time for this." He shook her hands off of him and strode away.

"Asshole!" Bethany rose out after him.

Ash shrugged it off and kept moving. He didn't have the time or the patience to deal with giggling girls. He had to find Raven, and fast. Who knew what they were doing to her now?

When Ash finally returned to Raven's, the fire trucks and police had already dispersed from the scene of the crime. There weren't even any onlookers, though an occasional human would stop and stare at the burnt wreckage that used to be Raven's apartment.

Lucky for the other humans who lived in the building, the human forces had been able to stop the fire from spreading to the other residences. It was always a bit tricky to keep a fire contained. Ash had had enough experience in covering Roth and his tracks over the years. By now he had it down to an art.

Ash casually strolled up to the building, acting as if he belonged there. His senses were on high alert, searching for any sign of the angels who had caused him to destroy his mate's home.

With the area clear, he ducked into the building and stalked up the stairs. His nose wrinkled at the odor of burnt metal and stone. Being who he was, one would think he'd be used to the scent of charred destruction. This was different. This wasn't some rando's place or somewhere in Hell. This was his mate's home. The one person made for him in all the universe. And he'd been the one to destroy her precious things.

Ash shot a glance down the stairs before pushing what was left of her front door out of the way. It crackled and fell apart beneath his hand. A cloud of dust and wood hit his face. His eyes watered and his nose tickled before he let out a loud sneeze.

"Damn it." Ash rubbed the long sleeve of his shirt under his nose and moved farther into the room.

His gaze found the metal of what was once the couch in the living room. The blackened and melted edges of the framework stuck to the concrete floor, its wooden planks burned to cinders. Ash could imagine Raven sitting on that couch, talking and laughing with Lily not more than twenty-four hours ago.

It felt like a hand clenched around his heart as grief and anger set in. No. He wouldn't let himself think that way. Raven wasn't dead. Not yet.

Ash moved through the wreckage cautiously, sniffing here and there as he searched for some clue of who had taken Raven. An angel was the obvious culprit, but which one? Had it been that psycho Gabriel? Or some lowly angel looking to get in good with the uppers?

He smirked. Like any of those wimps could take a badass like Raven. She wouldn't let them leave alive, let alone take her.

Unfortunately, that meant it had to have been one of the archangels. Someone with clout. Perhaps her father Michael.

Walking into the bedroom, his gaze found a charred but mostly whole fuzzy violet sweater. It lay underneath what was left of the bed frame, surprisingly unscathed. Thanking whatever third-world country had made it for using iffy materials, Ash scooped it up and brought it to his nose.

Inhaling deeply, Ash lingered over the scent of Raven. For a moment, Ash had been worried it'd been one of Lily's things. If he was going to find Raven, having something of hers would make it easier to track her scent. Not that Ash could ever forget what his mate smelled like. Still, he liked having something.

Holding on to the sweater, he shifted around the room, searching for the other scent he knew would be there. He had caught a faint whiff of it in the living room earlier. The angels. He hadn't been able to tell if it was part of Raven or her captors. Now, he followed it through the apartment and into the bathroom, where it filled the room more heavily.

Rage poured into Ash, and he barely contained his beast at the thought of some filthy angel touching his mate while she was in the bathroom. All kinds of what-ifs began to whirl through his head. His beast fought against his human form, snarling and scratching to get out and find the culprits.

The hellhound in him was too strong, too angry to contain for long. Ash's skin split and his bestial form took over. Smoke and mist spread around him, his skin covering in fur and fire puffing from his mouth and nose. His long claws dug into the concrete, leaving deep gouges in their wake.

They'd feel pain like they were no doubt causing his mate right now. He'd make sure of it.

A chilling howl filled the air as Ash burst from a fourth-story window and raced across the nearby roofs. He'd find Raven and kill anyone who got in his way.

. . .

Raven

A ragged scream ripped from Raven's throat as the searing pain sank into her abdomen. Arms stretched out to either side, Raven pushed against her bonds, refusing to cower. She gritted her teeth as tears burned her eyes, glaring up at her captor.

A malicious grin graced the otherwise handsome angel before her. Dark brown hair fell over a pair of gleaming blue eyes. Had he not been torturing her, Raven might have admired his beauty more. Gabriel had always been one of the more attractive angels. When he wasn't carving someone up.

"Come now, this can all end when you tell me what I want to know." Gabriel cleaned the blade in his hands with slow precision. Why he bothered to clean it when he planned to stick it back in her, she didn't know.

"Fuck you," Raven bit out, spitting at Gabriel. The bastard sidestepped it with a frown.

Clucking his tongue, Gabriel shook his head. "If only your father could see you now. Consorting with demons. Hiding the heir from us." He sighed, his disappointment evident. "A traitor to your own kind."

Raven kept quiet, knowing conversing with him would only goad him. Instead, she imagined all the ways she would rip that smug expression off his perfect face. Maybe she'd peel it off slowly with a cheese knife. A quick death was too good for him.

"Are you even listening to me?" Gabriel growled, waving his dagger in front of her face.

Holding back a wince, Raven shrugged. "Not particularly."

Gabriel bared his teeth, moving in so the bite of his blade pressed against her collarbone. "You have been spending far too much time with that half-breed whelp. It has made you far too insolent."

Ignoring the pain, Raven leaned closer to Gabriel and hissed, "That demon is ten times the being you could ever be. At least he doesn't have to tie up his women to get laid."

A muscle in Gabriel's jaw ticked, and for a moment, Raven thought she had struck a nerve, that he would give up his questioning and return to the torture. Anything was better than making small talk.

To Raven's dismay, Gabriel pushed off her with a huff. Twisting his blade in his hands, Gabriel stared beyond the stone walls of her prison. Not all of Utopia was puffy clouds and rainbows. There were places like this, just as dark and dank as the pits of Hell.

"What? No comeback?" Raven chuckled. "Who knew that the great Gabriel would be rendered speechless by little old me."

"No," Gabriel drew out, tapping his lips with his blade. "I'm thinking of the best way to break you."

Raven scoffed.

Gabriel turned to her, a brow arched. "You think you cannot be broken?"

She didn't respond.

His lips curled up in a secretive smile. "Everyone can be broken, Raven." He slid the flat of the blade along her chest, his eyes trailing after it. "It's just a matter of finding out... what makes them tick."

Swallowing hard, Raven hid her fear behind a defiant glare.

Gabriel let out a sadistic laugh. "Oh, this is going to be fun."

Roth

"Come now, you can do better than that," Roth taunted Lily with a frown. "Have you forgotten all of your training already?"

Lily scrambled back to her feet, her clothing covered in the training field's dark red dirt. She swiped a hand over her face, leaving a streak across her cheek. It would have been cute had she not already irritated Roth to the point of wanting to pull her over his lap and spank her pretty ass until it turned just as red as the dirt on her face.

"I'm trying." Lily readjusted her stance, her eyes flashing with annoyance. "Bitching at me doesn't help.

"This is not bitching," Roth explained, preparing to come at her once more. "This is simply reminding you of your true potential. You are wasting it with those half-assed attacks." Anger flared in her gaze. "Now come at me like you want to kill me."

"Oh, I'm going to kill you, all right," Lily muttered under her breath, thinking he couldn't hear her.

Lily held her arms out wide, her brow furrowed in concentration. Power thickened the air as a burning ball of light grew before her. Roth watched in anticipation, quietly cheering her on. They'd been at this for weeks now, and his love was nowhere near ready to face the angels or take on ruling the whole of Hell.

"You are taking too long," Roth criticized, dropping his stance. "You cannot expect your enemies to stand here and wait for you to power up like some kind of Power Ranger."

Lily's expression faltered, her lips twisting into a smirk. "You know what a Power Ranger is?"

"You're getting off topic, Lily." Roth narrowed his gaze on her. "You must focus." He held his hand out in front of him. A ball of energy formed in his palm within a second, burning black and red. "You must train your power to come when beckoned." He closed his hand over the ball of power and snuffed it out. "It should be as easy as breathing."

"I'm trying. I really am." Lily huffed

and dropped her arms. Her fireball flickered and then went out altogether. She dragged a hand through her violet hair. He was so happy she had dropped the glamour on her appearance, even if it made her even more irresistible.

"Not good enough." Roth walked toward her. "Utopia will not wait for you to be ready. They will come when you least expect it. If you are not ready—"

"Yeah, yeah." Lily waved him off, frowning as she wrapped her arms around herself. "It'll be Lily a la king for dinner."

"You are not taking this seriously." Roth stopped before her, grabbing her by the shoulders. "It is not only your life at stake. We are all relying on you to take up the mantle. To do what your father could not. What your mother sacrificed for."

Those perfect blue eyes narrowed into slits. "I know that."

"Do you? Because it seems like you are perfectly content with wasting time here." Roth's grip tightened on her shoulders. "Did you forget about Raven? Are you just going to leave her to the mercy of the angels? They could be slicing into her like warm butter. Ripping her wings from her back and trampling on her soul. All to find you."

Lily vibrated beneath his hands, her skin turning warm and then hot in a matter of seconds. "Of course, I do," her voice hard and terse.

"I don't think you do. Do you know what angels do to their own kind when they are guilty of treason?" Roth leaned in and lowered his voice to a harsh whisper. "First, they pluck the wings from their backs one feather at a time. Then they ravage their bodies the way a dirty, deviant human would." Fingers tightening on her shoulders until his nails bit into her skin, Roth finished with, "Then, when they are finished with them, they toss them to the cherubim so they may devour their flesh until there is nothing left. Is that what you want for our friend?"

"No!" Lily screamed, and a blast of scorching heat hit Roth in the chest, knocking him across the training fields.

Roth didn't immediately rise, the very breath knocked from him as his chest burned.

"Roth!" Lily rushed to his side, kneeling down to worry over him. Her face contorted in concern as she took in the damage she had done. "I'm so sorry. I didn't mean. I mean, I—fuck, are you okay?"

Wincing, Roth pushed up to his elbows and forced a smirk. "Now, that's more like it."

"Damn it, Roth." Lily smacked him

on the shoulder, making him groan. "Oops. Sorry. But seriously, I thought I really hurt you." Her lower lip pushed out as her gaze dipped down to her hands.

Unable to bear her unhappiness, Roth concentrated on the injury, using more energy than he should to heal it in a matter of seconds instead of hours. He lifted his hand to her face, tilting it toward her. "I'm fine. See." He took her hand and placed it on his bare flesh where the fireball had burned through his shirt. "I heal. No harm done."

Lily's fingers slid over his skin, tracing where the wound had been. Roth forced himself to stay still, the simple exploratory touch of her fingers making his cock harden.

"Was it all a lie?" Lily asked after a moment, her eyes meeting Roth's.

"What?" Roth asked, focusing on her face and not the pulsating need in his slacks.

Lily's eyes glistened with emotion. "What you said about Raven. Would they really do that to her?"

"Oh, baby." Roth wrapped her up in his arms, his arousal long forgotten in the face of her fear. "Raven's Michael's daughter. The angels are ruthless, but they aren't likely to defile *her*."

Her small hands clutched the front of

his shirt, her face buried into his chest. "And the cherubim?"

Roth smoothed his hand over her hair and back, making soothing sounds. "They are quite real. However, I highly doubt they have a taste for angel flesh." Roth smiled against the side of her head until she calmed.

"Good," Lily clipped out, and then punched him in the gut.

Doubling over, Roth released her to hold his stomach.

Lily stood over him, her hands on her hips. "That's for using my fear for Raven against me for training, asshole." She spun on her heels and stalked away from him.

Even though he was in pain, Roth grinned.

Lily

Motherfucking sexy bastard. How dare he use Raven against her like that? Lily slammed the door to her bedroom behind her, kicking one boot off and watching it sail across the room then hit the opposite wall with a satisfying thump.

The palace was less fire and brimstone than Lily had initially thought it would be. Walls made of shiny black and white marble spoke elegance and refinement rather than torture and death. Even her room was that of a high-class socialite. A four-poster bed made of shimmering pure white stone, not unlike the marble walls, held a mattress that felt like a cloud and gave Lily the best sleep she'd had in all her twenty years of life.

She dropped her clothing as she made her way to the bathroom, ignoring the red dirt that marred the otherwise pristine white floors. At least they had adapted to modern plumbing. Lily would have hated to have to live with cold showers for the rest of her life. If what Roth said was true, it would be a long one.

The door opened behind her. Lily didn't turn, still pissed off at Roth. She went about preparing her bath. Putting in some bath salts one of the servants had provided—from the boiling sea of turmoil, they had informed her—Lily pretended Roth's eyes weren't searing into every inch of her body. At the same time, she placed a towel near the edge of the tub.

Stepping into the tub, she sank slowly down, letting out a moan as the waters enveloped her worn and tired muscles. Roth growled low in the back of his throat. Lily promptly ignored it. Let him suffer.

Over the weeks they had been there,

Roth had been true to his word. They had kissed and cuddled. They had gotten to the point where Lily was ready to rip both of their clothes off and ride him until the Underworld froze over before Roth would promptly put her aside and race from the room. It was enough to make any woman insane.

Lily pushed her thoughts away from her aching folds and focused on washing. She was mad at him anyway. Even if angry sex was only slightly better than makeup sex. At least, that's what she had heard.

A virgin soon to be the queen of the Underworld. Lily sighed to herself. What a fucking joke.

Roth's presence moved closer to the bath, his boots clicking on the marble floor. Something heavy fell at his feet. Lily's gaze jerked up from soaping her arms. Roth had taken his shirt off, and the whole impressive expanse of his lickable abs was now on display for Lily's greedy eyes to see.

"What do you think you're doing?" Lily's fingers tightened around the sponge in her hands, her eyes riveted to the man in front of her.

"Taking a bath." Her breath caught seeing Roth's hands on his belt. Never had she watched someone remove their belt with such fascination. Licking her lips, she realized she was staring and shook her head, forcing a frown on her face.

"No, you're not. I'm still mad at you." Reluctantly, she tore her eyes from Roth's distracting figure and focused on the water harder than she had focused on anything in her life.

The metal of his belt clanked on the ground. Lily pressed her thighs together. *You're mad at him, remember? How could you still want to fuck him right now?*

Lily's libido did not give one shit about what Roth had done to get her to attack him correctly. It just wanted to know what he felt like all wet and slippery against her.

Roth's shadow fell over her bent form. Her head slowly lifted, and she was eye to eye with his cock. His massively thick and perfect cock. Her mouth fell open but when Roth chuckled darkly, she snapped her mouth shut and turned her face away from him.

The water moved behind her. Lily's shoulders stiffened even as every inch of her ached to find Roth in the water. One muscular thigh and then another encased her on either side. Her pride told her to get out of the bath. That if he wouldn't let her be mad at him, then she would just leave. However, the other part of her that had dreamed of having him this close to her, let alone naked with her, was begging her to say fuck pride and take what she wanted.

The feel of Roth's fingers trailing down her spine made the decision for her. She shivered at his touch. Perhaps she had gone about this all wrong. Instead of coming after him, she should have been trying to make him seduce her. Decision made, she held back a moan as those fingers found the curve of her ass and the other hand joined them. Roth cupped her hips in his hands and dragged her the short distance until her back was flush against his front.

A gasp escaped her throat. Hard and hot against her, proof of Roth's desire pressed into her lower back. Lily turned her face to the side, hiding her reaction in her hair.

"Are you going to be angry with me forever?" Roth's hot breath hit her skin, causing her to grab the edges of the tub just to keep herself from rubbing against him like a cat in heat.

"Perhaps," she answered curtly.

Roth brushed her hair over one shoulder, exposing the other to place wet open-mouthed kisses along her aching flesh. "Is there anything I can do to persuade you otherwise?"

The hands on her hips made small

circles, teasing close to her pubic bone, though never entirely passing that point.

Biting her lower lip, Lily closed her eyes tight. When Roth's mouth found a particularly sensitive place behind her ear, her body rebelled, grinding back against him. An answering rumble from Roth's chest followed by his hands cupping her breasts was almost more than Lily could bear.

Her head fell back against his shoulder at the tweaking of her nipples between his calloused fingers. Her thighs spread of their own accord, wanting nothing more than for those nimble fingers to find a home between them. When Roth simply continued his assault on her neck and breasts, Lily let out a frustrated growl and slipped a hand beneath the water.

Lily's fingers were just shy of quelling the throbbing in her clit when Roth grabbed her wrist. "Let go," she groaned in desperation. "If you won't touch me, then I'll do it myself."

"You know I cannot."

"Won't, you mean?"

Roth growled, not releasing her. "Do not press this, Lily Star."

"Oh, I'm going to press something," she countered and jerked her wrist from his grasp. "And don't forget who was the one who started all this. I didn't climb into your bath. You climbed into mine."

Shifting away from her, Roth sighed heavily. "My apologies. It was my mistake." Before Lily could protest, Roth was up and out of the tub, leaving her in the now-cold water.

She stared after his wet, naked figure with longing, but it quickly turned to irritation. Lily slapped the water and sank back into the tub. *Damn it.*

Ash

Why couldn't he find her? Ash had looked everywhere on Earth and the Underworld. Yet he couldn't find any trace of Raven.

He'd tracked her scent across the continent and all the way to the United Kingdom and then lost it. They must have known she was with a hellhound. How else would they know to twist their path in such a convoluted way, making him doubt his own nose?

Ash was at his wit's end. It had been months, he was nowhere closer to finding Raven, and it killed him inside. What were they doing to his mate right now? Was she dead?

No. Ash shook his head, leaning against the edge of the brick building he'd stopped at. Raven was his mate. If she were dead, he'd know it inside. His mate was alive and kicking some angel ass, hopefully.

There was only one place Ash hadn't checked.

Utopia.

Those winged narcissistic bastards were good at one thing, at least. Keeping the portals to Utopia hidden. Ash would have to hunt down one of those dickwads and somehow sneak into one of their portals.

"Still haven't found one little Nephilim, have you?"

Ash growled in the direction of the voice. "Do not talk about my mate that way. And no, I haven't."

"You're as useless as you are ugly, mutt." Warog stepped out of the shadows.

Sliding a hand through his already tousled hair, Ash flashed a mean grin at the bald-headed, tattooed freak. "Oh, Warog, I didn't know you thought about me like that. No offense, but I don't swing that way. I have a mate."

"Who you can't find," the fucker pointed out.

The beast inside of him howled to be released so he could rip a new hole in the smug demon's face. Ash's chest vibrated with suppressed rage, smoke billowing out of his nostrils as he snarled, "You think you can do better, Warog?"

"As a matter of fact, I do." Warog

crossed his arms over his over-muscled chest. "I happen to know exactly where a portal to Utopia is right now."

The beast in Ash withdrew, his interest in retrieving his mate far greater than kicking Warog's ass. "You… do?"

"Yep." He grinned like the cocky fucker he was.

Shoving his hands into his chinos, Ash cocked his brow. "Well?"

Warog busted out laughing, his hands on his hips and his head thrown back like a melodramatic TV villain. "Like I'm going to just tell you."

Scowling, Ash asked, "Are you serious right now? This is life or death, and you're going to hold out on me like some kind of dick."

Warog grinned. "Yep."

Ash couldn't say he was surprised. Warog was a good warrior. A good demon. But wanting any kind of decency toward other beings, even a celestial being, was asking too much of the brute. Squaring his shoulders, Ash narrowed his gaze on the ugly fucker. "Fine. What do you want?"

Warog picked at his nails, acting nonchalant when Ash wished he'd just spit it out already. Finally, after Ash was about to rip his head off and find Raven himself, Warog said, "I want a seat at the table."

Brows furrowed, Ash mulled over what Warog had said. "A seat at the table? What table?"

"You know what fucking table, mutt," Warog growled, stepping into Ash's personal space. His dark eyes glared down at him as if that were supposed to make Ash know what the Hell he was talking about.

Table. Table. Then a light bulb went off in Ash's head. He arched an incredulous brow at the demon. "You don't mean a seat at the poker table, do you?"

Warog crossed his arms over his chest and glowered.

Roth and a few of the other demons have a long-standing poker night once every decade. They gather around and shoot the shit while betting the only thing of value in Hell: territory. Not that Ash had ever had much to his name. Still, the game proved useful for gathering intel and favor among the other demons. Why Warog would want to sit in with them was beyond Ash.

Huffing a laugh, Ash shook his head. "Why would you even want to play with us? You hate us." Except for Roth, anyway. No one would dare say they hated Roth. At least, not to his face.

Maybe Lily would. The thought of the little spitfire made Ash's lips tick up.

"You think you're so funny, mutt?"

Smothering his laughter, Ash allowed the twitch to form into a full smile. "I think I'm fucking hilarious. That's beside the point. Why do you want to play with us?"

"Why else?" Warog poked a meaty finger at Ash's chest. "To gain territory of my own."

"But you have the...." Ash trailed off and frowned. "Where do you live, Warog?"

"None of your fucking business. Do we have a deal, or does your precious Nephilim mean so little to you?"

Warog's words struck a protective nerve in his beast, causing a low growl to escape Ash's throat. "Fine. I will tell you when the next one is. Now tell me what you know."

"Nuh-uh." Warog shakes his head. "I want to know now. How do I know you won't conveniently forget?"

Gritting his teeth, Ash bit out, "I don't know where it will be. It's not even the end of the decade yet."

Warog's thought skittered over his face. If he was that bad at hiding his emotions, he would be in for a rude awakening at the game. Maybe Ash would end up coming out the winner on both sides of this deal.

"Very well," Warog grunted before

holding his hand out. "But I want a life oath."

Ash stared at Warog's hand with obvious disgust. "A poker game is hardly worth one's life."

"But it's worth your Nephilim's, isn't it?"

Unable to argue with him, Ash slapped his hand into the demon's larger one. Magic skittered into his skin as a reminder of his promise. Holding back a wince, Ash withdrew his hand and shoved it into his pockets so as not to rub it in front of the other demon. "Now your part."

Warog's lips curled up into a vicious grin, making Ash think for a brief moment that he wasn't going to tell him until the next poker game. Then much to Ash's relief and horror, Warog leaned forward and sneered, "The top of the Eiffel Tower."

Damn it.

Roth

"I am aware of how dire this situation is." Roth leaned back in his chair, one leg crossed over the other. "But I will not send her with you. She's not ready."

A frustrated growl ripped from Ash's throat. "There won't be anything left of Raven if we wait until Lily is ready. Why don't you ask Lily if she thinks she's ready?"

Roth placed his glass down, not spilling a drop of its amber liquid, and leveled Ash with a stern glare. "Because I know what my mate would say. She would jump at the chance to risk her life for Raven's, regardless of the consequences. There is a bigger picture at stake here, Ash. I will not risk it... not even for you."

Ash flipped the table in a rage, sending its contents crashing to the floor in a scatter of glass and metal. "That's not good enough," he roared at Roth, smoke seeping out of his nose and mouth as his eyes turned to fire.

Roth calmly stared up at his longtime friend. He knew what agony Ash was going through. Roth would be in the same position were Lily missing. Roth would go through the fiery pits of Hell to save Lily if he had to. All things considered, Ash's actions were fully warranted, and yet....

"Roar all you like. Destroy the place. However, it will not change my decision. I will not put my mate in harm's way for the hope of getting through a portal to Utopia." Ash opened his mouth to interrupt Roth. He held a hand up, cutting the hellhound off. "I understand your desperation. However, would you trade Lily's life in exchange for Raven's? Would you ask that of me?"

Ash frowned, his anger wilting on his features. He flopped back into his chair and dragged a hand through his hair. "No. I wouldn't." He turned his head to the side and huffed out a breath, watching as leftover smoke rolled out. "What am I to do, Roth? Raven is within my grasp, and I can't do anything about it." A pain-stricken look crossed his face. "I keep imagining what they're doing to her. The pain they are causing her. I never should have left her alone."

"You will get her back, my friend." Roth tried to reassure Ash. "If anyone can find her, it is you. After all, you found my mate." His lips curled up in a slight smile as his eyes wandered to the woman walking into the room.

"Speak of the she-devil." Ash grinned at Lily, who groaned and dramatically collapsed onto the floor between them. Ash leaned forward and snickered at her prone figure. Her ass was looking particularly delectable today in her tight-fitting shorts. "What's wrong? Being the princess of Hell not everything you thought it would be?"

Lily lifted a hand and flipped him off before turning toward the destroyed table. "Did someone throw another temper tantrum?"

Ash scowled and sat back in his seat. "Your master won't let you help me get to Raven."

Her violet head of hair popped up in interest. "Get Raven? Did you find her? And whose master?" She crawled to her hands and knees. A position Roth would have been happy to take advantage of had she not been glaring at him. Even so, he might have to make an exception....

No. She's not yet of age. It would be wrong. And yet so right.

Internally, Roth groaned, uncrossing and recrossing his legs, turning to the side slightly to hide his growing need for his mate.

"What our dear friend is leaving out is that he has not yet found Raven. Only a portal to Utopia."

"Where they are holding Raven," Ash interrupted.

"Where you think they are holding Raven," Roth pointed out in a warning tone. "You are not sure, and I will not risk all our lives on the uncertainty. As I said, she is the daughter of an archangel. They will not kill her."

Ash gripped the arms of his chair, his fingers turning to claws. "But they would torture her. Are you saying that her pain is not worth the risk, only her death?"

"I'm not saying that at all." Roth held back an impatient huff at his friend's distress. "I am saying we are unsure of her whereabouts, and exposing Lily to the angels before we are ready could unravel all of our planning. I am sorry to say this, but we have to think of the many, not just one person."

"Hey, don't I get a say in this?" Lily shoved to her feet and kicked the side of Roth's chair with one booted foot. "Raven is my friend too. If I can help her, even a little, I want to."

Roth's amber gaze lifted to his mate's. "And how pray tell do you think you can help? All you can do is cause a distraction, or worse, be captured yourself. Then all of this, Raven's sacrifice, the lives of those human girls, your mother, would all be in vain. Could you deal with those consequences?"

Lily frowned. "No. But I also can't sit idly by when I could be doing something to help her."

"You are," Roth explained. He took her hand in his and drew her close, bringing it to his lips, where he brushed it along her knuckles. To his satisfaction, a small shiver shook her shoulders. "Being here and training, preparing yourself for the fight that is sure to come, that is your task, your responsibility. As it is mine to make sure you are ready."

"But Ash needs our help." Lily shifted

toward the hellhound. "We can't just leave him to fend for himself."

Ash stood and stretched, patting his stomach with a lopsided grin. "Don't worry about me, princess. I'll be fine. I'm used to taking care of things myself. Besides—" He flexed his biceps and struck a pose. "—no piece of winged garbage is going to get by these bad boys."

Lily giggled, the sound making Roth's heart soar. He was glad that his friend could cause his mate such joy. Lucifer knew she needed some happiness to break up all the strenuous training Roth had been putting her through. As he thought on it, it dawned that he should do something nice for her. A celebration for coming so far in her training. Lily turned that joyful expression in Roth's direction and he was lost. He never had much of a chance to begin with.

Lily

Lily's smile flashed across her face in bemused delight. "Where are we going?" Roth held her hand wrapped in his, leading Lily along the palace corridors.

"Just come along," Roth instructed.

Clutching his hand, Lily craned her head from side to side as she looked around the part of the palace she hadn't been to yet. "Aren't we going to train?"

"Not today." Roth squeezed her hand slightly, his lips twitching on one side. "Today, we're going to have some fun."

Brows furrowing, Lily watched Roth's face for any sign of what he had planned. Since Ash came by, Roth had been on edge, making her train harder than ever. Lily thought Roth felt guilty for refusing Ash.

Lily understood how he felt. She

wanted to get Raven back as much as Ash did. Okay, maybe not as much. If it had been Roth, Lily would go to the ends of the Earth and even Utopia to get him back. Of course, Ash would be the same. She hoped that her friend was doing okay. Lily tried not to think about what could be happening to Raven right then. It was hard enough having to train so much. If she dwelled even for a second on what Raven might be going through, she'd be consumed by it and wouldn't be able to focus on what was in front of her.

Still, if she were the praying type, Lily would be sending all her prayers to Raven.

Swallowing thickly, Lily's eyes dropped to the floor. *Please be okay, Raven.*

"What is it?" Roth asked, pausing in the hallway.

Shaking her head, Lily angled her face away so he couldn't see the tears threatening to fall. "Uh, nothing. Something got in my eye."

"Lil Star." When Roth said her name like that in his deep baritone voice, it did things to her insides. Except this time, it only made her feel guiltier. Here she was with her mate about to have fun while Raven was... was....

A gentle hand took hold of her chin, turning her face toward his searching amber eyes. Lily tried to avoid his gaze. If he kept looking at her that way, like he would do anything for her, she'd definitely cry.

"My mate, why do you ache so?"

Lily stared at his lips. Those perfect lips that knew just how to kiss her. Which were now pressed into a firm line. "Look at me, Lily Star."

Taking a deep, shuddering breath, Lily lifted her gaze. And that was all that was needed for the waterworks to start. Big fat tears rolled down her face, and she quickly moved her face to the side to wipe them away with the back of her hand.

Roth stepped closer to her, taking her in his arms as he rested his chin on top of her head. "Please tell me what I can do. It pains me to see you this way."

Lily clutched the front of Roth's crimson button-down shirt, pressing the side of her face against his chest. "Is there nothing we can do for her?"

He held her for a moment, not answering her question. Smoothing a hand down the back of her head, he pulled away and peered down at her. "There are some things we cannot control no matter how much we wish to Until you can keep yourself safe, all you would be doing is giving them another hostage."

"But I could—"

"Do you think Raven would want

that?" Roth asked before she could argue more. "If you went to save her only to be captured yourself? And they won't just keep you for questioning like they would with her. You are of Hell, while she is one of them. They would delight in killing you as slowly as possible. That, I could not bear. Do not ask this of me."

Pressing her lips together tightly, Lily jerked a nod. "Okay." She breathed out shakily. She plastered a smile on her face and stepped back from him. "So, where are we going?"

Roth's eyes softened, knowing that she was forcing herself to smile. "I thought we might see the rest of the palace. We've spent months here, and all you've seen are the training grounds and your quarters. But there is so much more to see."

"Oh," Lily answered, her interest piqued as they began to walk again. "I figured the rest of the palace was occupied by others or, like, not open to outsiders."

Chuckling in a way that had her heart skipping a beat, Roth glanced at her. "The daughter of the King of Hell is hardly an outsider."

Lily shrugged a shoulder. " I still feel like I don't belong here. I've never really belonged anywhere."

Roth jerked them to a stop and

placed his hands on her shoulders, staring deep into her eyes. "This is your home, and don't think for a second you don't belong here. You belong more than anyone else. And as for being occupied by others...." Roth trailed off, dropping his hands and moving once more. "Besides the servants, we're the only ones here anymore. The rest have scattered to the winds."

Frowning, Lily cocked her head to the side. "To the winds?"

"Some to the other rings of Hell, some to Earth or other worlds," Roth gestured off in different directions. "When Lucifer was taken, some tried to take over the palace, but some of the other loyalists and myself held them back until eventually, they gave up and left."

"Loyalists?"

Roth smirked at her. "You think Ash and I are the only ones who were anticipating your return? You have legions of demons waiting for you to lead them against the angels."

Lips pushing together in confusion, Lily searched the corridors. "Then where are they?"

Lifting an elegant shoulder, Roth said, "Hiding, training, waiting for the moment you are ready to lead them."

"And when will that—" Lily's head jerked to the side, her words lost. Roth tried to continue walking even though her feet had stopped. Her gaze bored into a set of double doors near her. More than twice her height, the doors were black and deep, sucking in the light around them rather than reflecting her image back. Lily walked toward one of the doors, both hands reaching for the handle.

She vaguely heard Roth say her name. Lily could barely hear him. It was as if she were underwater and sinking fast. The pressure weighed down on her, making her very bones ache as her hand wrapped around one doorhandle.

The door opened easily, like it wanted her to enter. The rest of the room was as soul-sucking as the material of the door. The ground and the walls were made up of that deep black stone, yet the room had an unnatural light. Lily's boots echoed around her as she made her way into the large room.

A dais stood in the middle of the room. The room was empty of anything else, even windows, other than a three-foot-high obsidian pedestal sitting in the center of the dais and the object it held. It called to her. The gleaming object was the very heart of the room. A living, breathing crown of metal and precious stones. Its voice whispered in her ears.

Take me. Love me. You will be queen, and all will bow down to your greatness.

Closer and closer she came to it. Her hands reached to take it. It was hers, after all, wasn't it? She was the heir. Why shouldn't she have a crown so beautifully crafted?

Yessss, it hissed to her. *That's it. Just a bit more.*

A hand clamped down on her arm hard enough to bruise. The sudden pain was enough to pull Lily's attention away from the crown, a low growl rumbling from her throat, her eyes narrowing on Roth. She opened her mouth to order him to let her go. He didn't give her a chance.

"You aren't ready yet, my love." Roth's words came out soft but firm, a warning in his tone. The hand on her arm led her toward the door, the pulsing words of the crown whispering at her back. Her head turned. "Don't look back." Roth's command had Lily whipping back around to him, keeping her eyes straight ahead.

Once they were out of the room, the doors closing with a resounding slam that echoed in her very soul, Roth kept moving. Each step away from the door eased the pressure on her bones, the whispering no more than a hum by the time they stopped.

When they stopped, Lily gasped as if breathing for the first time in several minutes. "What was that?"

Roth released her arm and turned, "That was something I had hoped not to expose you to until you were ready." His brow furrowed in thought for a moment. "Though, it is interesting how strongly it calls to you. It didn't even call your father quite so much, and it was created specifically for him."

Lily frowned. "That's my father's crown? Why did it call to me?" She wrapped her arms around herself and shuddered. "It was in my head. Whispering. I couldn't stop myself. I had to have it."

Inclining his head, Roth touched the side of her face. "The mantle of Hell is heavy and would crush any soul unworthy of its power."

His words sinking into her, Lily stared at him, crossing her arms and cocking her hip to one side. "Are you saying I'm not worthy?"

Brows lifting, Roth reached for her. She stepped back. Roth dropped his hand and sighed. "In no way am I saying you are unworthy. I am simply saying that you're not ready to fight the power behind the crown. I fear it will overtake you if you try to wear it before you're ready."

"Oh." All the defensiveness in her drained away at the real concern in Roth's eyes. Clearing her throat, Lily pushed a smile to her face. "So, where were we going before it became a *Beautiful Minds* kind of deal?"

Roth laughed, taking her hand. "I do not think the Wicked Crown would like being referred to as a film, but it does fit."

"The what?"

Glancing back at her as he began to lead them away once more, Roth said, "The Wicked Crown. The crown from which all Hell's power originates and will one day be passed on to you."

Lily couldn't help herself. Her head turned, and her eyes searched behind them, looking for any sign of that light-eating door and the crown that waited behind it.

Lily

The crystal lake sparkled in the rising sun, warming Lily's heart as she sat on its bank. Three years. It had been three years since Roth had brought her to Hell, and still, she felt as if she had barely made any progress. Three years of daily training, of sentinels coming back without news. The angels had been silent, barely even showing up on Earth. What was going on? It was hard to hold on to hope—hope to see Raven whole and in one piece.

Lily still couldn't hold her own against Roth. It was a rare day indeed when she ended up on top. And not in the fun sense. As he'd promised, he barely ever touched her.

She let out a heavy sigh. She hadn't made much progress in that aspect either. They were getting to know each other, and Roth was becoming one of her closest friends, but she wanted more—needed more.

Roth kept her at arm's length except for the occasional make-out session when the sexual tension became too much for them both. Those usually ended with Roth running away right when things got good and leaving all the heavy lifting to Lily's fingers.

Speaking of her mate, Roth was probably freaking out. He wasn't fond of her going off on her own, but she needed a break. A break from training. A break from the tension between them. Even more so, a break from the constant whispering of the Wicked Crown.

Ever since the first time she laid eyes on the Wicked Crown, she couldn't forget it. It woke her in the middle of the night. It pulled at her every time she walked by the room. It had become so bad that she avoided that part of the palace as much as possible.

She picked up a nearby rock; it was smooth like obsidian, its dark surface reflecting her tired face back at her. She let her fingers slide around the edges of it, frowning at her reflection before tossing it into the water.

Small at first and then out, out, and out as far as Lily could see, the whole lake rippled from her little rock. She couldn't help seeing parallels between it and her. She hardly thought she was that significant, and yet the angels and even the demons believed she was worth killing for. Destroying worlds for.

Lily tensed, her brow furrowing.

It was quiet.

Hell, she had learned, was not unlike Earth in some aspects. They had small creatures, birds, lizards, and such, even if they were nothing like she had ever seen before. Yet, it was never completely quiet. There was always a hum of life around her.

Now, there was nothing. No chirps. No hissing. It was as if even the air had stilled.

The ground rumbled beneath Lily's fingers, the pebbles around her bouncing around like beans in a hot pot. Scrambling to her feet, Lily went on alert, her eyes scanning the area for whatever had caused the sudden hush.

She pushed magic into her hands, remembering the lessons Roth had taught her.

Be ready. Don't wait for them to attack first. The time it takes to get prepared, could have already killed you three times over.

Fire, her go-to magic, formed in her hands, whipping and swirling around her palms. Her shoulders tensed, her heartbeat erratic in her chest. After a moment or two when nothing happened, Lily lowered her hands and shook her head ruefully.

Paranoid. She was paranoid. It was all the pressure of training that had her thinking everything was out to get her. Either way, she should head back.

Shoving her hands into her pockets and scuffing her boots on the ground, she shook her head once more before turning her back on the lake. Lily didn't even make it a step away from the lake before the world shook and an ear-splitting roar pierced the morning.

Hands covering her ears, Lily spun around, her eyes going to the lake where a long-necked monster covered in multi-colored scales shot at least five stories above the surface, sending a tidal wave of water toward her.

She automatically lifted her hands and pushed the wave away from her so she didn't get swept away. Though judging by the size of the monster in front of her, she probably would have been better off being taken as far away from it as possible.

The beast opened its mouth, revealing razor-sharp teeth as it let out a piercing scream once more, the beady eyes on either side of its head searching for its prey. Lily debated staying as still as possible and hoping it didn't notice her, or just running. Roth had warned her of the creatures of Hell. Not all of them were like him and Ash. Some were nothing more than beasts that relied solely on instinct. Feed, fight, fuck. Lily didn't want to be on the receiving end of any of those.

Deciding the best course of action was caution, Lily inched back from the lake's edge, her hands up and ready to fight if need be. The monster continued to search for whoever had dared disturb it, except it didn't seem to have very good eyesight. Its bloodshot eyes kept sweeping past where she stood as if it couldn't see her. The realization made her bolder.

Quickening her steps, Lily was almost at the tree edge when something snapped beneath her foot. She winced as the monster turned its attention to her, its large mouth roaring once more as it narrowed in on her position.

Well, at least she knew its hearing worked.

For a millisecond, Lily debated running or staying and fighting. If the monster kept to the lake, then she could quickly get away and not risk her life at all. However...

The creature didn't particularly want to wait for Lily to make up her mind and moved swiftly through the water, making the water lap at the shore. Its long neck turned into a bulky body covered in scales and spikes down its back as it came out of the water.

Okay. So not a water-bound monster.

The decision was made for her. Lily spun on her heel and took off through the trees, hoping to lose the monster in the thick woods. The white trunks of the foliage did nothing to hide her vibrant purple hair. To her dismay, the beast crashed through the trees as if they were nothing more than a nuisance.

Lily's foot caught on something, and she went down, hands scuffing on the ground, the sting of skin breaking making her hiss. The monster was even closer now; Lily didn't take the time to check her wounds before she scurried to her feet and was off again. It wasn't until she came face-to-face with a large expansion of rock that she stopped.

A dead end.

Panic set in, and she didn't have time to worry about how she had gotten turned around before the creature was upon her.

"Shit, shit, shit," Lily hissed under her breath, her eyes darting from side to side, feeling very much like a mouse caught in a trap. Every step closer made Lily's heart pound harder. It was when it was only a few yards away that Lily realized this was what she'd been waiting for. This was her test to see if she was ready. If she could face down this beast, then surely she could handle the asshole angels who were after her.

Solidifying her stance, Lily prepared for an attack. Her hands came up in front of her, her powers building in her core, running through her veins and making every inch of her skin tingle. The air around her shifted, lifting her hair off her shoulders and fluttering her clothes around her.

The creature hesitated. It cocked its head to the side as if curious about what kind of being Lily could be.

Not giving it the chance to attack, Lily pulled her magic into her hands, creating balls of fire and launching them at the creature. The monster rocked back with each hit, letting out a roar of distress. As far as Lily could tell, her attack wasn't doing much damage, if any. Not letting up, Lily switched the fire out for wind, hoping to push the beast far enough away that she could make a run for it.

Where are you, Roth? she screamed in her head, hoping their bond would convey her difficulty. She hated to be the damsel in distress, but she was out of her element. So much for this being her chance to prove her mettle. Dammit!

For all she knew, the beast could only

be killed by a magical sword pulled out of a virgin's ass. If she'd learned about this creature before, she couldn't remember a thing right now in the thick of the action. Eventually she would run out of magic and need to recharge, and that would be when the monster made her its lunch.

The wind didn't do much but irritate the beast, so Lily wrapped her magic around one of the trees, ripping it from the ground and using it to beat the monster back. It whimpered and then growled, snapping its sharp teeth at the trunk. Thankfully, the trees were made of stronger stuff than back on Earth. The claws swiping at them didn't even dent the bark, nor did the strong jaw clamping down on them.

Soon she found herself in a tug-of-war with the beast, its sharp teeth holding on to one of the trees while Lily tried to get it back from it. Lily had never had to use so much power in this manner, and she could feel herself weakening. If she couldn't deal with something like this, how did she expect to fight a legion of angels?

She couldn't. If she didn't die here today, then she was as good as dead once the angels got a hold of her. If she was lucky.

Refusing to admit defeat, Lily shoved another gust of wind at the beast, pushing it back a foot or two. For a brief moment, Lily was distracted by a dark shadow cast from overhead. The lapse was what the beast needed to get the upper hand. It threw the tree trunk away and came at her full force. Lily braced herself for impact, knowing this was the end.

A tug at her center made her pause and look up at the sky once more. Roth. Her mate. He was here.

Black wings arched from his back as he barreled down to the ground, throwing himself between her and the beast. Roth didn't bother to pull back when landing, causing the ground to shake and crack at his weight. His pale hair whipped around his face as amber eyes locked on to her, no doubt surveying every inch of her for injury, before turning the heat of his gaze on the monster.

"*Stop.*" The one word halted the stampeding creature.

Its claws dug into the ground as it pulled up short of hitting her mate. Lily gaped as the creature laid its head on the ground and whined. It freaking whined at Roth like he was its master, and she was the new toy it wanted to play with.

Roth glanced away from the creature to Lily and asked, "Are you all right?"

Dumbfounded, Lily nodded and

winced as her scraped hands touched her sides. "Yeah, for the most part. How did you... how did you do that?"

Roth ignored her question, taking one cautious step after another toward the creature, making sure not to spook it. Lily gawked at her mate as he placed a hand on the creature's head and murmured in another language. After a moment or two, he patted the side of the creature's jaw and stepped back.

The creature reared back to its full height and gave Lily one more resentful look before turning back the way it came. Water splashed in the distance, and the woods came alive once more.

Walking over to where Roth stood, Lily stared down the long line of trees the monster had destroyed and then to Roth. "What just happened?"

Roth's jaw tightened, and his eyes were hard. He'd never looked at her in such a way before. Was he... mad?

"We will discuss it at home." Roth pulled her into his embrace, his wings pushing them up and into the sky without another word. It was all Lily could do to keep hold of him and not look down as Roth swept through the air, leaving the mess of her ordeal in their wake.

Roth

When Roth landed on the balcony of the sitting room, the few servants scattered. Putting his wings away, rage pounded through Roth's veins as he clutched Lily to his chest. Anger at himself for letting her out of his sight and at her for wandering off alone. And underneath all of it was a perpetual fear.

The what-ifs swarmed his mind. What if he hadn't gotten there in time? What if Lily had been cold and broken in the traitor's woods? He didn't know if he could handle it. The image of her lifeless body on the ground. Those beautiful blue eyes staring up at him without her usual spark, void of life. Her lovely skin ashen and cold from death's touch. Roth shuddered and held her tighter to him.

"Roth," Lily's voice was muffled against his chest. Roth ignored her protest, hugging her. Lily let out an indignant sound and shoved him away. "Roth, you're going to suffocate me."

Not releasing her, Roth allowed a small distance between them. "It would serve you right after the hell you put me through."

Lily stared at him. "Hell? What hell? You mean the constant training and hovering? Never giving me a moment by myself?"

His lips twisted to the side. "I am simply trying to prepare you for what's to come. I do not want to send you out there unprepared and have you end up like... well, like what almost happened today." Roth scowled and gripped her arms. "Do you know how close you were to death? If I hadn't come, that hydra would have happily eaten you whole. I'd be lucky if there was anything left to mourn."

Lily's lower lip pushed out, her eyes downcast. "I had it under control."

Roth released her before he did something he regretted. "Clearly." He walked away from her and to the bar set up on the east wall. He poured himself three fingers of brandy before downing it in one gulp and refilling his glass.

"I did. I was figuring it out. Which you never let me do," Lily growled, and she might as well have stomped her foot on the ground to express her indignation.

Unfortunately, the reminder didn't serve to cool the fire in his blood. All he wanted was to take her and claim her as his own. To lay the final mating mark upon her and maybe, just maybe, the unending need to protect her would lessen.

Turning around, Roth stalked back over to her. "What I do is to protect you. How can I give you more responsibility if you can't be trusted with the amount you have now? You ran off in the middle of training and didn't even tell me where you were going." He swung his arm between them, the dark liquid in his glass sloshing over the rim.

Lily had the decency to flinch. "To be fair, I didn't even know what I was doing. I couldn't very well tell you. And if you hadn't been playing dirty, I wouldn't have run off in the first place. Using my attraction to you against me, knowing full well you weren't going to follow through." She flipped Roth off and turned her back on him.

Before she could get two steps away, Roth grabbed her with his free hand. "Don't you walk away from me. You may be the heir to Hell but that doesn't mean I won't put you across my knee right here and now."

The scent of Lily's arousal nearly knocked Roth off his feet. Not that he could tell by the stiffness in her shoulders. Despite the glower on her face, it only grew lovelier with each shade of red it turned.

She jerked her arm out of his grasp and hissed, "You wouldn't dare."

Smirking, Roth leaned in. "Try me."

Lily let out a shuddering breath, her chest heaving between them. Then, as if they had planned it, they moved as one. Roth's glass shattered on the ground as his fingers slid into Lily's hair, tangling in her violet curls. Lily grappled at him as well, wrapping her legs around his waist and tugging on his hair. Their mouths collided in a fight for dominance, each of them wanting nothing more than the chance to be that much closer to the other.

Roth dropped one hand down to Lily's backside, the alluring scent of her arousal turning his cock to granite. He practically threw them against the nearby table, knocking the vase of flowers to the ground. Neither of them glanced its way.

Lily tugged at Roth's shirt, pulling it out of his pants and sliding her nimble fingers beneath. Each touch of her fingers sent an electrifying need through him.

More. More flesh. More touching. More tasting.

Releasing her mouth, Roth placed open kisses along her neck, sliding his tongue down the column of her throat until she let out a startled gasp. He locked his mouth over one spot and devoured her with skilled precision. He faintly heard a pop, something scattered, and then those seductive hands were touching every bit of his heated skin.

Roth lifted his head long enough to say, "That was my favorite shirt."

Lily's lust-filled eyes flicked up, her lips curled in a mischievous smile. "I'll get you another one."

His lips twitched, then in one swipe of his hand her own shirt split at the seams, becoming nothing more than scraps of fabric.

Lily frowned at the shirt and then up at him. "You're playing dirty again."

Roth slid his finger along the line of her bra strap and down along the cup hiding her breast from him. "Do not pretend you do not enjoy it." Another flick of his hand and her bra joined her shirt in the scrap pile.

The most wondrous sound escaped Lily's throat as her back arched and her nipples tightened under Roth's gaze. What glorious breasts they were. Never in all of his immortal life had he ever seen breasts as perfect as his mate's. The generous handful, the dusty pink of her nipples, and the cute little gasps she made every time he flicked one of those pert tips. It didn't take Roth long to taste them.

His tongue swirled around one peak before giving the same attention to the other. They had to be treated fairly, of course. Roth could no sooner pick a favorite breast than a star in the sky. If he spent the rest of eternity worshiping Lily's breasts, Roth wouldn't complain.

Except there was another part of her that beckoned him like a siren. The flowery, musky scent of her need grew with each flick of his tongue and scrape of his teeth. Roth only had their shared dreams as a reference, but if having her breasts in real life was this magnificent, he could only imagine what tasting her sweet hot center would do to him.

"Please, Roth," Lily gasped, her fingers pulling at his long ashy hair. "Don't stop. I swear I'll die if you do."

A low chuckle escaped his throat at her neediness. He couldn't let that happen. With the same precision as he sliced apart her top and bra, Roth disposed of her pants, leaving her in a tiny, sheer pale pink thong. A deep growl unlike any he'd made before rumbled as the scent of her arousal permeated the air.

Lily shamelessly spread her legs for him, begging for his attention.

Lowering himself to his knees, her

soaking wet center sat at his eye level. Perfect. They were perfectly made for one another. If there was any other evidence needed this was all the confirmation Roth required right here.

Roth's cock twitched in anticipation. He pushed thoughts aside and pressed his face between her thighs. Lily's breath caught as Roth buried his nose against the thin fabric of her panties, breathing in every inch of her arousal.

"By the depths of Hell, you are delicious," Roth murmured against her core. He slipped two fingers beneath the fabric and trailed them up and down her slick folds, enjoying the small whimpering sounds coming from Lily before pulling the fabric to the side. There was the very thing that plagued his dreams and waking hours. Untouched by any other man or woman. His. And only his.

Male satisfaction filled him.

Lily's hand tightened on his hair as she grumbled, "Are you going to stare at it all day or lick me?"

Roth's gaze drifted up to her face. Lily's cheeks were flushed becomingly, her eyes dilated to their fullest extent and an impatient frown on her lips. Keeping his eyes locked on hers, he allowed his tongue to dart out and just barely stroke across her folds. Lily's eyes squeezed shut and her lips parted with an, "Oh."

Mine, his mind screamed as he lapped at her folds more fully. *All mine.*

Finding that little bundle of nerves, he paid close attention to it, savoring every gasp and moan that came from his mate's mouth. He had dreams of having her like this, spread out beneath him in ecstasy, just a moment away from cascading over that cliff. The only thing that would have made this better would have been to release his painful girth from his pants and sheathe himself inside of her, to sink his cock into her as he sealed the mating mark on her. Making the twenty-two years of her wretched life fade away and leaving only him.

As if a bucket of cold water had been dumped on him, Roth jerked away from her tantalizing center, wiping the remnants of her sweetness off his face. "I need to go." He backed away, his hands up as if he would undo what had been done. Roth tried to look anywhere but at the heavenly vision of his mate on the precipice of pleasure. "This... this shouldn't have happened."

"Wait, what?" Lily murmured, jumping off the table. Her legs wobbled underneath her, making a part of Roth smirk with pride.

He squashed it down, shaking his head. "No. I'm sorry. I forgot myself for a moment. This"—he pointed a finger between the two of them—"won't happen again."

Before Lily could reach him, he bolted for the balcony, released his wings and took to the air. Lily's wrathful screams followed after him. Roth ignored them, pushing harder, faster. Anything to get him as far away from the mistake he'd almost made as fast as possible.

Ash

"I'm not sure this is a good idea. Why can't you get Roth to help you?" Marchocias, one of the marquises of Hell, asked for the tenth time, his midnight blue skin helping him blend into the night.

"Shhh," Ash hissed, peering over the edge of the railing at the base of the Eiffel Tower. "You're going to attract their attention." His eyes darted to where the angel scum hovered a few hundred feet from the top of the Eiffel Tower. He'd tried everything he could think of to get past the guards to the portal to Utopia, and failed every time. This was his last hope. He'd desperately gone to Marchocias for assistance even though Ash might have been better off going it alone. Yet there he was, dancing with torture and death for the sake of his mate. If she was even alive.

Ash winced at the thought and shoved it away. He wouldn't think that way. He'd know it if Raven was gone. Three years on Earth was not the same thing as three years in Utopia. She could have only been there for a few days or weeks. It was that thought that kept him from completely going insane with the need to get to her. Any other thoughts and he'd have already committed suicide trying to get past the guards himself.

"So, what's the plan?" Marchocias nudged him with his elbow.

Huffing a sigh, Ash pointed up at the top of the tower. "You are going to fly up there and get their attention, draw them away from the portal long enough for me to get in, and then take off."

Marchocias bobbed his head. "Got it. I can do that." Then he frowned. "But what if they catch me?"

Rolling his eyes, Ash shifted into position. "Don't get caught."

"But what if—"

"For Hell's sake!" Ash hissed at Marchocias. "You're the fastest demon in the seven rings; you can handle a couple of winged assholes. Or should I go tell the rest of your brothers you wimped out without a fight?"

Marchocias scowled. "Don't you dare. I'm no wimp. Just cautious." He rolled his shoulders and stared confidently at the angels above. "All right. I'm ready."

Ash patted him on the shoulder. "That's it. You got this. Now... go!" he gave Marchocias a bit of an encouraging shove to get the demon going before taking his position back up. This was it. His last chance. If he couldn't get in this time, he didn't know what else he could do.

The smaller demon spread his wings, the leathery dark blue skin of them resembling that of a bat's, and pushed off into the sky. Ash kept track of the demon as he pushed his wings faster until he reached the top of the Eiffel Tower. The two guards circling the tip froze in midair, watching his approach. Marchocias stopped a short distance from them and yelled obscenities in their direction before turning on the wind and darting away. The two guards stared at him for a moment and then glanced at each other before taking off after him.

Now.

Ash morphed into his hellhound form and clambered up the metal frame of the Eiffel Tower, pushing his legs to move. He had to reach the top before they came back, or all of this was for nothing. He wouldn't let this be it. Ash would get to her. He'd save Raven if it was the last thing he did.

Just as Ash reached the top of the

tower, a shout came from behind. Ash didn't look back. It could have been Marchocias being cut down, it could have been one of the angels coming back to take him out, he didn't care. All that mattered was getting through the portal and to Raven. She was all that mattered.

His powerful legs pushed off the top of the tower and toward the shimmering air in the sky. Passing through the portal would have been easier if he had wings but since he wasn't of the winged variety of demon, he had to rely on this impressive jump to get him there. Thankfully, the portal was only a few dozen feet from the top of the tower and he easily hit the shimmer and found himself vaulting out the other side.

Ash's body hit the dirt and grass, rolling over and over until he anchored his massive claws into the ground to slow his momentum. Heaving a breath, Ash remained alert. He didn't have time to rest. Someone would have no doubt noticed he'd come through the portal. Most everyone had alarms for trespassers nowadays regardless of who guarded the damn things.

A cluster of trees laid a short distance from the portal entrance and he made for it like a shot. Once he was in the clear, he'd change form and be able to better blend in with the locals. He'd still have to keep the glamour over his energy, or the angels would know exactly where he was as soon as they came within a hundred feet of him.

Under the cover of the trees, Ash shuddered and stood on two legs again. His gaze shifted and took in the world around him. Utopia. How many demons could say they had actually been there? His lips quirked up at the edges. At least now he knew what all the fuss was about. Utopia was a virtual paradise with its bright skies and green plains. Even the trees were perfect. He leaned against the trunk of one, letting his fingers shift into claws to scratch down the surface. The bark reformed almost instantly behind his marks.

He huffed. "Too perfect."

Glancing around him, he checked for a way to the main palace. He had no doubt they would take Raven there. She was the archangel's daughter, after all, and a traitor. It would be prudent to keep her under heavy guard. However, getting to the palace might be a bit trickier than getting into Utopia.

The trees only covered a small area before the rolling plain took over once more and then there was nothing to hide him from the angels' sight. The palace sat a short distance away, its pointed turrets shining in the two suns.

Two suns? Ash covered his eyes as he stared up at the sky. Of course they couldn't just have one. They had to have two. What assholes.

Shaking his head, he wandered along the edges of the copse searching for the perfect vantage point before he set out across the plains. He'd have to wait until dark or risk exposure. As much as he hated to admit it, there was no other way. Ash glared up at the two suns, one slightly ahead of the other. If there was any dark to wait for.

Hold on Raven, I'm coming for you.

Raven

Something zinged inside Raven, and it wasn't the three knives currently lodged in her chest cavity. Gabriel had a knack for getting them in just the right place, going for pain, not the kill.

Still, whatever it was kicked her out of her pain-induced sleep and had Raven peering around the room. Who knew how long they kept her here—it could have been weeks, days, or even years. It certainly felt like the latter. Raven didn't know how much more she could take. If only Gabriel would kill her. Unfortunately, the sadist got off on her pain too much and wouldn't give her the satisfaction.

Groaning, she tried not to make too much noise lest she attract her captor's attention. Gabriel had left her just as she'd passed out from the blinding agony of being skewered three ways to Sunday. She highly doubted he'd come back between then and now. He preferred his victims awake so he could hear them scream.

Raven leaned her head against the wall behind her and shifted her shoulders, trying to get some circulation back into them. God, what she wouldn't do for a massage. Hell, while she was making wishes that weren't going to come true, Raven might as well wish for someone to save her, or at least bring her a cheeseburger. Starvation might not be on the list of ways to die, but it didn't keep the hunger pangs away.

A howl ripped through the air. Raven's head jerked to the side. She hissed. The movement caused one of the knives to grate on her bones.

She didn't know why she cared about some dog howling. It wasn't like Ash could come for her here. He was a hellhound, not an angel. He'd have to be completely void of intelligence to think about coming after her on his own.

Her lips pursed. Well. She never pegged him for a genius. Perhaps he....

Raven shook her head. No. She was

not going there. False hope would do her no good. She'd have to find her own way out of here. Raven winced and glanced down at the knives sticking out of her chest. Just as soon as she figured out how exactly to do that.

The door to her prison swung open and Gabriel's malicious grin appeared. "Oh good, you're awake." He stepped up to her, sliding his fingers along her bare chest before wrapping a hand around one of the hilts sticking out of her. "Let's pick up where we left off, shall we?"

Gabriel twisted the knife. Raven's scream echoed off the walls and she clenched her teeth, preparing for another long day of torture.

Lily

Arms crossed, Lily stomped through the hallways of the palace. She hadn't heard from Ash in weeks and every time she asked Roth about it, he just said, "Don't worry about it. Worry about your training."

Lily snorted. "Worry about your training," she mimicked to herself.

"Your Majesty?" A servant stopped in the hallway next to her. "Are you all right?"

Lifting her head, Lily startled at the sparkling midnight skin of the servant. Holding a silver tray in a three-fingered hand, the servant tilted its horned head to the side, its full black eyes blinking at her. Lily couldn't tell if it was male or female though it was completely nude, its whole body smooth from chest to... well... crotch. The servant cleared its throat and Lily jerked her eyes back up to its head, a blush coming over her cheeks.

"Sorry," she mumbled. When the servant didn't leave, Lily tightened her arms across her chest. "Uh, I'm fine. Just thinking out loud."

The servant smiled, its sharp teeth startling. "Do not be distressed. We've seen you in the training yards. You have nothing to worry about."

Lily dragged a hand through her hair and turned her head to the side, blushing even more. "You have? Wait." She dropped her hand and frowned. "What do you mean 'we'?"

The servant didn't even seem embarrassed as it said, "All of us, of course."

"All of you?" Lily's eyes widened. "How many of you are there?" She glanced around the hallway feeling as if she were being watched at that moment.

Giggling, a very feminine gesture, the first gender-identifying trait the servant had shown, the servant stated, "Oh, quite a few. How many exactly, you'd have to ask Prince Roth."

Lily arched a brow at the formal title. Three years and Lily had rarely seen a servant, and those she had seen were very much humanoid like herself and none of them had deigned to speak to her.

Shifting in place, Lily tucked her hair

behind her ear, wondering how to bring up the subject of what exactly the servant was. Lily didn't know why it bothered her not knowing if the servant was male or female. A name would have helped her adjust.

"Bacchii," the servant said out of nowhere. At Lily's questioning expression, the servant continued, "My name is Bacchii. I'm a succubus."

Lily's eyebrows hit her hairline. "I'm sorry, you're just not what I expected a succubus to look like. You're so...." she trailed off, waving a hand at the shimmery black surface of the female demon.

Bacchii smirked and her skin rippled. In place of horns, long flowing ebony hair fell down to her butt and her skin changed into a less reflective shade. Supple breasts formed underneath a tight crimson dress that barely covered whatever genitalia she had going on beneath that flimsy piece of fabric.

"Better?"

"Wow," Lily gaped at her voluptuous form. "Can you change into anyone?"

Shrugging an elegant shoulder, Bacchii's skin shifted again and Lily was looking at herself in the mirror.

Eyes wide, Lily leaned toward Bacchii, scanning over every feature. "Does my nose really look like that?"

Bacchii giggled, covering her mouth with Lily's hand.

Disturbing.

"What's going on here?" Roth's voice boomed through the hallway.

Lily's head jerked toward him, scowling. "What does it look like? We're talking." Lily gestured to Bacchii, who had transformed back into her normal genderless self. "Now look what you did."

Roth didn't even bother to look at Bacchii as he stalked toward her. "You're supposed to be working on your levitation, not keeping the servants from their jobs."

Bacchii bowed to Roth and quickly excused herself.

Lily reached out toward her retreating figure. "Wait, Bacchii." Then she huffed, jabbing her hands onto her hips as she swirled back around. "What is your problem?"

"My problem," Roth snapped, closing the distance between them, "is how you are constantly neglecting your duties. How do you expect to face the angels when you keep wasting your time with... with...." Taking a deep breath, Roth swung his arm in the direction of where Bacchii had left. He dropped his arm and let out a long sigh. He rubbed his forehead with the other hand.

Lily's anger dissipated as she took in

Roth's expression. Closing the distance between them, she took his hand in hers. "Everything will be fine, Roth."

Roth clutched her hand with his and met her gaze, a small smile creeping out. "When did you become such an optimist?"

Lily grinned and sidled up to Roth's firm chest. "Well, I have to be, with you leaving me with a constant lady boner. There's an orgasm in the future kind of thing." She pulled her lower lip between her teeth and peered up at him from beneath her lashes.

Roth lifted their joined hands to his mouth, pressing his lips to her knuckles. "My love, you are not the only one who has been in a constant state of torture. I want you more than breath itself. My veins burn with my desire to have you wrapped around my body."

Her own blood warmed at Roth's words, her thighs shifting against one another. "Then why do you make us wait?"

Brushing her hair away from her face, Roth lowered his lips to her forehead and pressed a chaste kiss there. "Come, let's go to dinner. Then we can discuss your progress today."

Blood cooling, Lily allowed Roth to direct her down the hallway toward the private dining room they used most nights. Stepping inside, Lily eagerly surveyed at the spread laid out on the table. Candles were lit and the lights were low, giving the room a more romantic ambiance, while the table was full of all the foods she loved from Earth. Triple meat pizza. Burgers from the restaurant down by the campus. Even tacos from the street vendor on Main.

"Do you like it?" Roth's breath brushed her ear.

Lily twisted around and threw herself into his arms. "Yes. I love it. How did you know?"

Roth held her close before leading her to the table. "I may have cheated and peeked into your head more than usual during our dreams. Also, Ash was rather forthcoming when I asked about you before."

Licking her lips, Lily didn't know where to start. Everything looked so good. She was going to stuff herself until she burst. She restrained herself long enough for Roth to help her into a nearby chair, then it was no holds. She grabbed whatever she could get her hands on, piling it all onto her plate while Roth took the seat next to her, a simple glass of wine in front of him.

"Aren't you going to eat?" Lily asked, a taco halfway to her mouth.

Roth shook his head. "No, this is for you."

Reluctantly, Lily placed the taco on her plate and twisted in her seat. "Why?"

"Because the grease on all this makes me want to run away screaming." He winked at her with a grin.

"No, I mean," Lily shifted closer. "Why did you do all of this?"

Roth's eyes twinkled with amusement. "Have you forgotten what today is?"

Lily picked a fry off a tray and chewed on it as she contemplated what day it was. The days had blurred together so much thanks to all the training and routine that had become her life that Lily couldn't for the life of her think of anything special that was supposed to happen.

"Uh... Hanukkah?"

Chuckling, Roth lifted his wine glass to his lips. "It's your birthday."

The fry got lodged in Lily's throat. Roth slapped her on the back until she spit the offending potato onto the table-cloth. Grabbing her wine glass, she swallowed some and then wiped her mouth with the back of her hand.

Lily cleared her throat and then croaked, "Thanks." Taking another drink, Lily leaned back in her chair. "Are you sure?"

"Quite."

She held her hand up and counted on her fingers, her brows scrunched together. "Oh, I guess you're right. Go figure." Lily lifted a shoulder and dropped it. Roth watched her as she picked at her plate, his attention making it impossible to indulge like she really wanted to. "You know, I don't usually celebrate my birthday. I told you that last year."

Roth twirled his wine glass between his fingers. "And as I told you, I wish to celebrate every year of your life for the rest of your life."

"More like count down until D-day," Lily muttered into her glass.

"D-day?" Roth smirked.

Lily let her lips tilt up as she speared her hot dog with a fork and lifted it to her mouth. "What do you think?" She bit into the hot dog and licked her lips slow and purposefully.

Roth set his glass down on the table and with a move quick as lightning, he pulled the remainder of the hot dog out of her grasp and downed it, licking each fingertip provocatively. Each slide of his tongue reminded her of his head between her thighs not a few weeks ago. His lips still wet from the grease of the hot dog, Roth slid his tongue along his teeth. "I think you are a tease, Lily Star."

Lily leaned forward until their

mouths were only inches apart. "Takes one to know one."

A growl shuddered against her lips before Lily was pulled out of her chair and found herself straddling Roth. She let out a surprised groan at the hard length nestled against her pulsating center. Hands on his shoulders, Lily shifted in his lap until Roth let out another delicious growl.

"Stop that," Roth commanded, his hands tightening on her hips.

"Or what?" Lily countered, rotating her hips once more for good measure. "You won't fuck me?"

Roth locked eyes with her, all the playfulness gone from his face. "Is the idea of waiting two more years really so horrendous?"

Lily's lower lip pushed out, her fingers trailing through his hair. "Isn't it for you?"

He stroked the pad of his thumb across her lower lip, pinching it gently between his thumb and forefinger. "Every second."

"Then what are we waiting for?" Lily lowered her head, pressing her forehead to Roth's. "The angels could attack at any moment, and who knows if we'll make it?"

"You will live if it's the last thing I do." Roth's eyes grew hard. "I will cut down anyone who dares raise a hand to you."

Lily shook her head, her hair creating a violet curtain around them. "You can't protect me forever. And what if you go first? Then I will always wonder."

Roth grimaced. "It wouldn't be right."

Nipping at his lips, Lily murmured, "I may only be twenty-three, but in my soul, with the weight of all of Heaven and Hell on me, I feel about a hundred and five." Roth opened his mouth to her.

Those strong hands lifted her by the thighs and sat her on the table before him, knocking over the wine glass. It shattered on the ground. Neither of them bothered to pick it up.

Roth pulled back from her kiss, brushing her hair away from her face as he kissed her eyelids, her nose, and then the corner of her lips. For a moment, Lily thought that he was going to leave her all hot and bothered again, then he was pushing up her shirt. Not wanting to break whatever hold she had on him now, Lily lifted her hands and kept quiet, except for the occasional moan and encouraging murmur.

Her bra dropped to the table on the pile of tacos. Lily didn't give two shits. She inched her hands underneath his shirt, quietly slipping the buttons out of each hole. Roth cupped her breasts, focusing her attention before she could take in his muscular bare chest. Arching her back, Lily locked her ankles around Roth's legs and pulled him closer.

The rough pads of his fingers slid between her breasts, trailing down to stop at the line of her pants. Lily lifted her gaze to Roth's as she mimicked his movement, playing with the waistband of his slacks. Her breath held as she waited for him to back off, to run away like he usually did when things got too heated between them.

Roth flicked the button of her pants. Lily did the same. The sound of her zipper going down reverberated in the large room. Lily swallowed and shakily pulled Roth's zipper down as well. Roth's pants dropped to the ground, his long, hard cock free. Licking her lips, Lily couldn't believe this was actually happening. After all the years of dreaming about this moment, they were finally going to have sex.

Suddenly, Lily was nervous. What if she did it wrong? This would be her first time. Was it Roth's? She'd never thought to ask and now that it was happening, she didn't want to stop it just to find out. Who knew when she'd have another chance like this?

"What is it?" Roth tilted her chin up. "Are you scared?"

"No." Lily shook her head, keeping her eyes on the planes of his stomach and not the size of his cock between them. "I just... don't want to disappoint you."

"You could never disappoint me." Roth captured her lips in a searing kiss, his hands going to her hips once more. She lifted them for him to remove her pants. It would have been overly sexy had she not had her boots on still. Roth didn't seem bothered though. He knelt before her, unlacing one boot and then the other, removing her socks along the way. Her pants came next, falling to the floor on top of his own.

Lily's legs spread farther apart, more than ready for him. Roth teased his fingers along the insides of her thighs, brushing along her slit. Lily's hips bucked toward Roth, the tip of him nudging against her soaking heat. She grabbed a fistful of his hair and jerked his mouth away from her neck, latching on to those tempting lips, her legs hooking around his hips to bring him closer again.

Roth reached between them and positioned himself, ripping his mouth from hers to ask, "Are you sure?"

Swallowing, her nerves completely taken over by her need to have Roth inside of her right now, she hissed, "Yes, yes. I'm sure."

Lifting her hips up, Lily reached back and planted her hand behind her. It landed in something squishy yet she didn't care because Roth's tip rubbed at her entrance, playing peek-a-boo with her center. Each brush of his cock made her breath catch and her heat quake. When he finally slid all the way home, Lily's head fell back with a gasp.

"Are you all right?" Roth paused to ask.

"Not if you don't keep going right now." She tightened her legs around him, urging him to continue.

With each thrust of his hips, Lily's thoughts became even more incoherent.

The table rattled and dishes fell off the sides, plates crashed, and all that precious food Roth had acquired for her ended up on the floor. A part of her wept for all the wasted food but the part of her that was currently getting her world rocked told her she didn't need to eat.

Roth grabbed one of her legs and lifted it up and over his shoulder. The angle became deeper and a sound Lily had never made before ripped from her throat. It was desperate and demanding. When Roth swiped a finger across her clit, her world tilted on its axis and everything exploded into multi-colored lights.

Her fingers dug into Roth's upper arms as he slowed his pace, dragging out her orgasm for as long as possible. Roth stiffened above her, a low rumble from his chest vibrated through her, and it all sent her even further over the edge.

Lily collapsed back on the table and winced. She met Roth's hooded gaze and laughed. "Oops."

"Yes," Roth glanced around them and smirked. "It does seem that we have quite ruined dinner."

Swiveling her hips in a motion that made both of them groan, Lily breathed out, "Believe me, this more than made up for it."

Roth leaned forward and licked the side of her face. "It was delicious."

Raven

⚜

A fist collided with Raven's jaw, the force of it nearly knocking her teeth out, cutting her lip and cheek. She should have been grateful. Raven's mouth would have been drier than the Sahara had it not been for the blood in her mouth, her tongue near to shriveling up into a dried mushroom. Though, for some reason, she couldn't find it in her to thank the gloating bastard.

Gabriel had gotten bored with slicing her up and had turned to brute force. He'd been using her as his own personal punching bag for the last half an hour or so. Today he didn't even bother to ask her any questions as a pretense for a reason to beat the crap out of her. He just came in swinging.

Raven almost preferred it. The endless pain. The mindlessness of it. No need to come up with some half-assed answer or witty retort. Maybe Gabriel had gotten tired of the game just as she had. Either way, she would take her lickings and hope he'd leave her be soon enough.

After a moment, Gabriel paused and frowned, lowering his bloodied fists. "You're taking all the fun out of this. Beg. Plead for your life. Something."

Turning her head, Raven spit, her eyes too swollen to see where it landed. "Sorry to disappoint," she coughed, her voice coming out a bare whisper.

"Ah," Gabriel mused, moving closer to her. "I see. I've been neglecting you. Here," he turned away from her briefly before something nudged her lips. Hesitant to take anything from her captor, Raven angled her head away. "Come now. It's just water. Of all the ways I could kill you, poison would be the least of them. What fun would that be?"

Unfortunately, Raven believed him. If Gabriel wanted to kill her, he'd make sure it was slow and painful. So when he pushed the cup to her mouth once more, she greedily gulped down the contents of it, coughing when she took too much at once.

"There's a girl," Gabriel cooed. "That's better, now isn't it?"

Raven tried to glare at him. "Fuck you."

Gabriel laughed. "Good. Let's continue. Where are they hiding?"

Turning her face away from him, Raven sighed. "Who?"

Stepping up close to where she was hanging off the wall, Gabriel grabbed her aching chin and jerked her face toward him. "Look at me when I'm talking to you."

"My apologies, your supreme assholeness." Raven smirked but it came out more of a wince.

"You're so much like your father." Gabriel tilted her face to the side and brushed his cheek against hers, his lips close to her ear. "He too just needed to be broken."

Raven jerked away from him as much as she could, making Gabriel laugh.

"Now," Gabriel cleared his throat and stepped away from her. "let's get serious. While playing with you has brought me great pleasure, the higher-ups want answers and they want them now. So, this will be my last time asking nicely before things get really ugly."

A harsh giggle escaped her throat. She couldn't help it. It was just so funny. "This was asking nicely?"

Gabriel practically beamed at her.

"Oh, dearest. I could do so many more delectable things to that lovely body of yours, but have held back in hopes you will cooperate." He leered, causing Raven's body to revolt. It took everything in her not to vomit right then and there. She had been thankful that Gabriel had resorted to physical pain versus psychological. Up until that moment Raven thought perhaps the bastard couldn't get it up, so torture was how he got his jollies off.

She hated being wrong.

Picking up a knife off the table of toys Gabriel had laid out, he scanned over her form with the calculated precision of a surgeon rather than a man about to use sex as a torture device. Perhaps he couldn't get it up after all. However, that left all manner of horrors awaiting her, making her wonder if she could get him to kill her now rather than later.

Before she could open her mouth to speak, there was a knock on the door.

Gabriel scowled and twisted around to shout, "What is it? I'm busy."

A muffled voice called through the door but Raven was too far away to pick out what they were saying. Gabriel, however, was not. He sighed and placed the knife gently back on the table before turning to her. "My apologies, it seems I have been called away. We'll have to pick this up another time." He approached her, cupping her chin in his hand. "Don't miss me too much." He pressed a hard kiss to her mouth, prompting Raven to jerk and snap at him with her teeth. Gabriel wasn't deterred and simply laughed. "Keep that fire. I do prefer an active participant to a dead fish. See you soon." He grinned once more before leaving, the door shutting with a resounding thud that made Raven's heart stutter.

She had to get out of here. There was no way in Utopia or Hell that she was going to let that sadistic asshat touch her again. Pain and blood she could handle—the thought of that jackass putting his putrid dick anywhere near her, she just couldn't.

Raven pulled at the metal of her restraints, trying to figure out if there was some way to leverage herself to at least snap the loop attaching it to the wall. Maybe if she twisted around?

Gabriel had been smart enough to chain her feet as well as her hands or else she'd have strangled him with her thighs already. It did make trying to turn around a bit harder. Thankfully, she had inhuman strength. Sadly, most of that strength was atrophied from wasting away in this shithole. Still, she had to try.

Shifting in place, Raven turned as much as her bindings allowed, which wasn't far. Shit. Unless she got her legs free, there was no way she'd be able to get enough leverage to break the cuffs on her arms. Raven stared at the metal around her wrists for a long hard minute.

She smiled.

It wasn't a pleasant smile. If anyone had seen her at that moment they would have run away as fast as possible. The diabolic wheels in her head turned as she twisted her hand, fingers pulling and tugging until a painful snap hit her ears. Raven bit down on her lip to keep from screaming out, not wanting to attract unwanted attention, as she jerked and contorted her hand until enough of the bones had broken to squeeze them through the metal cuff.

Whimpering over her poor hand, Raven slowly slid the chain through the loop on the wall. Her shoulders sagged and she let out a small sigh, rolling her them to loosen the limbs. Finally, she could put her arms down. She'd never complain about arm day again.

Tugging at her feet, Raven contemplated how she'd get out of those chains. She scanned the room before her eyes locked on the table with all of Gabriel's toys. Maybe if she leaned forward enough, she might just be able to reach it.

Holding her broken hand to her chest, Raven lifted one leg and angled her body forward, her uninjured hand reaching for the table's edge. She missed it the first couple of times, falling flat on her face. The third time she fell, she grabbed for the leg of the table and dragged it toward her. The legs scraped on the ground with a loud scuff. Raven winced but kept at it. It was too late to back out now.

Once she pulled the table close enough to her, she used the leg to lift herself back up to the table surface. When her eyes reached over the edge, she wrenched the nearest thing off the table, holding the crowbar poised and ready to attack the angel in front of her.

"You don't need that, Raven," her father, Michael, told her, keeping his distance. "I'm not going to hurt you."

Raven scoffed and held the crowbar up. "Like I'm going to believe that. No one here has done anything but hurt me my entire life."

Michael's eyes softened as he stepped toward her. "And it is my greatest regret that you had to suffer this long. Please...." He held his hand out to her. "Let me make it up to you."

Raven frowned, her brows furrowed. "You think I'm just going to hand over my weapon and trust you? How do I know this isn't some kind of trick?"

Pausing midstep, Michael mimicked her expression. "Ah, I suppose you don't."

He pursed his lips and then nodded as if deciding something for himself.

He walked around the edge of the room, going slowly, like she were some foal he didn't want to startle. Raven watched him with suspicion, her arms poised to attack if he so much as looked at her wrong. However, when her father stopped at the wall where her legs were still chained, he grabbed hold of the metal loop and pulled. It ripped from the wall, bringing with it part of the stone holding it there.

Raven snorted. "Thanks. Now I have something else to slow me down." She jiggled one leg and then the other, wanting nothing more than to collapse on the floor but knowing now was not the time to break down.

Michael knelt at her side, his eyes on her stiff form as he wrapped his hand around the cuff holding one leg. With another pull, it was broken. He did the same to the other leg, finally freeing her from her captivity.

"Why didn't you just do that in the first place?" Raven asked, staring down at the broken cuffs and then the large chunk of the wall sitting near it.

"Would you have let me get that close if I tried?" Michael countered before reaching for her uninjured hand. Raven gripped the crowbar tighter and backed away a foot. Michael dropped his hand and sighed. "I need to take that one off too, unless you'd like a leash to slow you down, as you say." His lips ticked up at the edges.

Raven's mouth twisted to one side, debating before holding her arm out to him. She had to trust him if she wanted to get out of here. Besides, he'd already seen her. She'd have to kill him either way to get out of there if this proved a trick.

"There," Michael exclaimed as she rubbed her wrist against her chest. "Now isn't that better?"

Staring at her father, she swallowed and said, "Yes. Thank you." Without another word, she turned to the door. She didn't know where she would go, but she had to get out of there. Maybe she could hide out in the lesser celestials' wing until the search for her died down. Then she could make for the portal to Earth and hopefully find Lily and the others.

"Wait." A hand landed on her arm. Raven stared down at it until Michael removed it. "I mean, where will you go?"

Raven clutched her injured hand to her chest and took a step back. "I'll figure it out. I always do."

Michael glanced down at her hand

and then up to her eyes. "You won't get very far looking like that."

Raven shrugged and made for the door once more. "I don't have much of a choice, now do I?"

"You could stay with me."

The words stopped her in her tracks. "What was that?"

Clearing his throat, Michael laced his fingers in front of him like a docile woman rather than an archangel, the right hand of God, all powerful and wrathful. "I said, you could stay with me. Until you recover, that is."

Raven's mouth dropped open. She snapped it shut and nodded once. "Okay."

Gabriel

Of all the idiotic things. He had to teach his underlings when something was an emergency and when it was a minor inconvenience. A hellhound in Utopia. How quaint. Surely, they could handle that on their own. What would they have Gabriel do? Offer it a bone and tell it to go fetch?

Gabriel shook his head and scowled as he stalked back to his home. He had just gotten ready to take things to the next level with the Nephilim. So far, he hadn't gotten much out of her. Actually, the only thing he had elicited from her were threats and snide remarks. She was a tough one, that Nephilim.

When he decided to make more children, Gabriel would have to ask Michael where he found his women. The ones he had procreated with before were not made of the same stern material. Worthless. All of his children were absolutely worthless.

Except one.

Gabriel sneered as he thought of the only child that had ever been worth a damn. The only child he had ever been proud of, and he had betrayed Gabriel to his cursed brother, Lucifer.

Astaroth. Damn Gabriel for ever spurting forth the seed that created that disappointment. If he hadn't been born, then Gabriel could have saved himself a lot of headaches.

It wasn't like he had ever mistreated his child. He gave him all that he could ever want. Women to lay with, a large home, servants, angels to lord over—and he had given it all up for those disgusting humans.

Even centuries later, the boy still had not come home. He stayed in Hell, of all places. As if that were better than Utopia. Everyone begged and fought to come here. So why would he want to live in that cesspool of a place?

Perhaps he had not given his son enough power. Lucifer had been quite taken with him. Still, Astaroth was Gabriel's child. One would think that would make Lucifer shun him. His brother never did care for him or his ways.

Well, if his son wasn't good enough for the King of Hell, then Gabriel would just have to make sure that the heir wasn't anything to write home about, either. Starting with the Nephilim that would help him find her.

Ash

A howl ripped from Ash's throat as a ball of holy fire singed his fur. Those damn flying fucks. Didn't they know how to go to bed at night like the rest of the universe?

So much for staying undetected. The moment Ash had darted into the open plains, the vultures had been on him like roadkill on a highway. He zigged and zagged through the fields, trying to keep from turning into fried hellhound. One would think living in the fires of Hell would keep him from getting burnt by the fires of Utopia. Apparently, they were a different kind of fire all together.

Ash's lungs burned as he pushed himself even faster. He was almost there. He could see the edge of the palace just in the distance. He'd get there and find Raven in no time. Then they could all go back to Hell, where it was safe.

Bet no one in their lifetime had ever said those words.

His amusement was cut short as a

bolt of lightning hit the ground right before him. He jolted backward and switched directions, snarling at the sentries in the sky. "Is that all you got?" he sniped at the air and laughed. Ash had to admit he hadn't had this much fun since Roth and he had taken on those insurgents in the fourth ring.

The side of the palace came into sight and Ash refocused his attention on it. Once he hit the palace it would be harder to keep a low profile, especially with dumb and dumber chasing him. He had to find somewhere to hide out until they gave up on him. Then he could search for Raven once more.

A dark shadow fell over him, the wind pushing him back. He dug his claws into the ground as he skidded to a stop in front of the winged being. Ash prepared to attack whoever blocked his way until he realized it was Michael, Raven's father. The ground shook with the force of his landing, raising Ash's hackles.

Another two thuds sounded behind him. Ash glanced back at the two sentries and glared. Damn, now he was surrounded. Enemies to the back, and well, he didn't know what to expect from Michael. He could be here to help with Raven's rescue or work against it. The archangel had never been one to show all his cards before.

Michael paid Ash no mind and stared over his head at the ones behind him. "I'll take care of this mongrel. Go back to your posts."

"But Sire, he's trespassing. Shouldn't we...?"

Narrowing his gaze on them, Michael asked in a dangerously soft voice, "Are you questioning me? Do you think I cannot deal with one lowly hellhound?"

"No, of course not. I mean, we just meant...."

"Go back to your stations before I make sure you are cleaning out the trenches instead." Michael's no-nonsense tone caused the angels to nod profusely before taking back to the sky. With only Michael and Ash left, the archangel turned his attention to him. "Now, what do you think you are doing here?"

Confusion furrowed Ash's brows. When he realized the archangel in front of him wasn't going to attack, a shudder ran through him, leaving him in his humanoid form. "Searching for Raven."

"She's being taken care of," Michael replied, his hands behind his back.

"But Gabriel took her, and you know how he likes to torture people. Especially traitors. There's no telling what he's doing to her." Pain clenched at Ash's heart, the thought of his mate at the hands of that maniac almost too much for him to bear.

Michael clucked his tongue. "Like I said, she is being taken care of. Go home." He waved a hand in Ash's direction before turning his back on him, like it was all decided.

Ash held his ground. "I won't leave her."

Sighing, Michael shook his head. "Do you really think I would not help my daughter? Trust me, she is safe, and no further harm will come to her."

"What do you mean, 'no further harm?'" A low growl rippled out of Ash's mouth. "What's happened to her? Let me see her. Now."

In a rush of air, Michael had Ash by the throat, his feet dangling above the ground. "Do not make demands of me, pup. You will leave this place before you too are taken and then I will have to explain to my daughter why her mate has been dismembered."

Ash glowered down at Michael before nodding his head once. "Fine."

Michael lowered him to the ground and then lifted a hand to one side. The air shimmered and swirled before them where there had been nothing before. "You may use this portal to return to your realm."

Ash stepped toward the portal. He hesitated.

"Go," Michael commanded. "Before I change my mind and let the sentries have you."

Swallowing, Ash stalked over to the portal and walked through it. He came out the other side right at the edge of Purgatory. Spinning around, Ash found the portal gone and so was Michael. Well, Ash supposed that could have gone worse for the first time meeting his in-law. He just prayed that Michael was telling the truth.

Michael

Hellhounds sneaking into Utopia? What had the world come to? In Michael's day, demons stayed in Hell and angels stayed in Utopia, where everyone belonged. And yet, his only daughter was the mate of that lowly beast.

Michael couldn't deny Raven her mate. Doing so would only make their relationship even more tenuous. She barely trusted him now to keep her safe. What would she do if he started telling her what to do with her life? He hadn't exactly been a model father.

No, he'd have to suck it up and let her make her own decisions, no matter how wrong they were.

"How are you feeling?" Michael brushed his black hair over his shoulder and peeked his head into the room he'd given to his daughter.

Raven sprawled out on the bed, her eyes resting on the ceiling as she clutched her bandaged hand. They were lucky they healed quickly, or else she would have been in worse shape by the time he reached her. It hurt Michael's heart to know that he had failed her in such a way. If only he had been there sooner.

"I'm fine. You don't need to hover." Raven's platinum bob shifted as she turned her head toward him. Those big eyes, still bruised and slightly swollen from her ordeal, narrowing on him. She looked so much like her mother.

Michael nodded, shifting to leave. His eyes found the tray by her bed, the food untouched. Frowning, Michael stepped farther into the room and approached the bed. He picked the tray up, his weight shifting to his back foot as he glanced at his daughter. "Was the food not to your liking?"

Without looking at him, Raven muttered, "I'm not hungry."

"I can hardly believe that." Michael snorted, taking a careful step in her direction. "You've been held captive for three weeks. That would be three years in Earth time. If you were human, you would have starved to death by now."

Raven made a scoffing noise in the back of her throat, still not looking at him. "It's a good thing I'm not human then."

Pausing for a moment, Michael looked down at the contents of the tray and then back to her implacable expression. "It's not poisoned."

No answer.

Michael sighed. "Why would I save you only to poison you? Do you really think so little of me?"

Raven's gaze finally landed on him, and he didn't like what he saw there. "I don't think of you at all. Not since you made it perfectly clear you wanted nothing to do with me when you left my mother to fend for herself."

Michael grimaced. "Your mother and I were unfortunate. I wish I could —"

"Stop," Raven interrupted him, sitting up and swinging her legs over the bed. "Just stop. I don't want to hear your sappy lamentations or regrets. Nothing you could say will change that I wasted the last century of my life wondering why my father didn't want me. So save it. I'm over it."

Not knowing what to say, Michael kept his mouth shut. In a way, Raven was like him too. Once betrayed, he never forgave or forgot. It did not bode well for their future relationship. However, Michael was nothing if not relentless.

"Nevertheless, I will not have it said

that I am not a gracious host. Please eat something. I can have something else prepared for you if you prefer." Michael arched a brow, waiting by her side. "Earth food, perhaps?"

Raven stared at him long and hard. Blowing out a hard breath that fluttered her bangs, Raven huffed a laugh. "You're not going to give up on this fatherly act, are you?"

Michael simply watched her.

"Fine. I'll eat." She grabbed the tray from his hands and placed it in her lap. When Michael didn't move, she scowled. "Well, I'm not going to do it while you are watching."

Inclining his head, Michael strode across the room and out the door, leaving it open. He didn't go far, though. Walking a few yards down the hallway of his home, Michael stopped and leaned against the wall, his ears angling back to his daughter's room. Perhaps he did not entirely trust her either.

When the sounds of utensils moving reached his ears, Michael relaxed slightly. Good. She was eating. Once she was fed, they could discuss what would happen next. He had no doubt that his daughter wanted to rush off to Hell to help her friend, the daughter of Lucifer.

Michael thought of the slip of a girl he had met back on Earth. Her hair had been an auburn color so unlike the royal violet of her mother and with startling blue eyes so suspicious and yet curious about his presence. When he first saw her, Michael thought he had been looking at her mother, Lilith, and yet there was a spark in her eye that was purely his brother's bloodline.

His gaze shifted out the nearby window, drifting toward the tower in the distance where he knew his brother's prison sat. Did he know? Had word reached him that his daughter lived? Surely not, or Michael had little doubt that Lucifer would have broken out of his confines. That mockery of a prison could not hold his brother any more than it would have kept him. It was probably one of the reasons why Gabriel and the others searched so tirelessly for the heir. They knew the moment that Lucifer found out she was alive, there would be hell to pay.

"Are you going to stand guard even when I shit?" Raven's voice jerked Michael from his thoughts. Standing in the middle of the hallway, her arms crossed over her chest, Raven appeared the very definition of a defiant child. It made Michael wish he could have seen her when she was smaller. Had she thrown such terrible tantrums? What was her first word?

Pushing his queries aside for later, Michael forced a smile as he turned to her. "I hardly think that is necessary. However, if you're anything like me—"

"I'm not."

Michael pursed his lips, holding back his irritation at being interrupted. After a heartbeat, he began again. "Would you like a tour?"

Raven arched a white eyebrow before dropping her arms. "Is this where you live?"

Nodding, Michael slipped his hands into the pockets of his slacks. "Among other places. However, while in Utopia, this is where I usually dwell." He stepped toward her, his gaze cautiously on her face. "It is your home now. If you'd like."

Not answering his question, Raven glanced around the hallway before stalking to the window. She peered over the edge of the jalousie window, searching the pale pink sky. "What time is it?"

"Barely dawn."

"Did you go out?"

Michael watched as she noted the extra sentries circling the sky. Keeping his distance, Michael approached behind her. "Yes. We had a trespasser late last night. But he has been taken care of."

"He?" Raven's face turned hopeful

before she controlled her features. "What was it?"

"A demon," Michael answered carefully. "A hellhound, to be precise." He monitored her expression, checking how deeply her affection for her mate went.

Her eyes widened a fraction, and she swallowed visibly. Though obviously interested, Raven's voice came out nonchalant, as if she were asking about the weather. "And what happened to him? It?" If Michael hadn't been watching her face, he wouldn't have caught the slight crack in her facade when she winced.

"I sent him packing."

Raven spun around so suddenly that they were toe to toe when her heavy gaze landed on him. "What do you mean, you sent him packing?"

Michael put more distance between the two of them as he shrugged. "Exactly what it means. I sent him home. I couldn't very well have a demon do what is a father's job."

Her eyes searched his face for a long time before she bypassed him and asked, "Do you have a training room in this place? I have the sudden urge to punch something."

Chuckling, Michael shook his head as he followed after her. Just like her mother.

. . .

Raven

Jaw clenched and eyes focused, Raven closed her mind out to everything else but the task in front of her. One, two. One, two. Each punch made a satisfying sting reverberate up Raven's arm as she pounded into the punching bag.

She had hardly left the training room since her father showed it to her. When she did, it was only to quickly down something to eat or shower. Then she was back to it.

Sleep eluded her most nights. Every time Raven closed her eyes, she feared she'd wake up to see it was all a dream. The fear that she'd wake up and find herself chained to that wall again with Gabriel standing over her was more than enough to keep her awake until the two suns rose over the windowsill.

The only time she found herself able to sleep was when she worked herself so hard that she could pass out from exhaustion. Even then, her dreams were fitful and full of screaming. Her screams. Raven would wake up in a sweat that only a cold shower would eradicate.

Her father was worried. She knew it. He hadn't exactly tried to be covert when he checked up on her. Whenever she went to the kitchen, he would offer her a piece fruit or ask how her night had been. Most of the time, she'd give him a one-word answer before going back to the training room.

Raven knew he was trying to get to know her. To make up for lost time. The problem was, Raven didn't have the energy or even the inclination to pretend she was interested. There was a war on the horizon, and she had to be ready. That way, when Raven came face-to-face with Gabriel again, she could give him a taste of his own medicine.

Grinding her teeth, Raven pummeled the image of Gabriel in her mind, growling out between blows, "How do you like it? Huh? How do you like it?" She jammed her knee into the bag and then spun around to do a kick. Overestimating her strength, the bag snapped off its hinge and shot across the room, hitting the wall with a loud thump.

"Feel better?"

Huffing, Raven spun around to see her father leaning against the side of the training room door, his black hair pulled back into a ponytail, and his usual slacks and button-down nowhere in sight. If she hadn't been so taken aback by his presence, then the sight of him in the form-fitting pants and tank top would have made her shudder—some things one should just not see on their parent's body.

"I was just going to shower." Raven began to unwrap her hands and headed for the door. Michael stopped her with a shake of his head.

"Nonsense. You've been beating that old bag all week and gotten nowhere. Don't you think it's about time you fight someone who can hit back?" Her father arched his brow, his stance daring her to say no.

Raven glanced back at the punching bag and then back to her father. Sucking on her teeth, Raven jerked her head in resignation. "Fine."

She followed Michael onto the training mats and took an offensive stance. Michael didn't even bother to position himself one way or the other, merely standing there as if he were about to have tea. For some reason, his nonchalance pissed Raven off.

Without asking if he was ready, Raven shot across the room, fist extended. Michael sidestepped it with a sigh.

"Sloppy."

Scowling, Raven swung her leg around, hoping to catch him off guard. Michael grabbed her leg with one hand and shoved it, causing her to spin to the floor. Raven wasted no time jumping back to her feet and coming at him again.

That time she let out all her anger. At Gabriel, at Michael, and, if she was honest, with herself.

Michael ducked and weaved, side-stepping every punch and kick she tried to land on him. It only made her fight that much harder. Finally, Michael stopped defending her attacks and began to push back. This time it was Raven's turn to go on the defensive.

Her father's punch hit her arm. Raven winced. *Fuck.* He hit like a truck. If she hadn't been a Nephilim, that would have broken something.

Shaking off the numb sensation coming over where Michael had hit, Raven didn't move in time to avoid his other fist as it came out and clipped her on the cheek. She went down to the ground, clutching her face and glaring up at the archangel.

"Had enough?" Michael stopped before her hands on his hips.

Rotating her jaw, Raven snapped, "Hardly."

Michael smiled, and for a moment, Raven swore she saw pride in his eyes. "Then let's continue."

Lily

Groaning, Lily turned her head in the tight grasp Roth had on her hair as he bent her over the dining room table. "What is it with you and this room? Every time we have a meal, you want to jump my bones."

Roth growled in her ear. "Are you complaining?" His other hand reached between her thighs and cupped her soaking sex through her pants.

Lily moaned and bucked her hips back against him. "Never. Just would like to eat my food before it got cold for once."

"No one is stopping you." Roth dragged his tongue along the line of her throat before playfully nipping at her jaw. "I have everything I need right here." He pulled at her hips until her ass was flush against the hard line of his zipper.

"Well, as satisfying as that is, I need

food a bit more substantial inside me," Lily laughed over her shoulder before letting out a long moan. Roth was a wicked, wicked man. "Okay, fine. Five minutes. Then I'm eating."

"We'll see about that." Roth licked the shell of her ear.

Soon Lily found herself without pants and Roth buried deep inside of her. She gripped the tablecloth beneath her and met each of his thrusts with a strangled scream. Ever since they had taken their relationship to the next level, Roth hadn't been able to keep his hands off of her. Not that she was any different.

During training, if they happened to get too up close and personal, the next thing she knew, they'd be rolling around on the dirt like a couple of animals. Roth looked at her for too long while they were taking a break in the library, and she was crawling into his lap, riding him until they scared away every servant within the vicinity. In fact, most of the servants had avoided them for the better part of last week. Lily supposed one too many of them had gotten more than an eyeful of their princess and prince of Hell.

While Lily couldn't complain about Roth's insatiable appetite, her stomach was rebelling against her. She just wanted a damn piece of bread. The item of her desire sat a few inches away from Lily's face. Except if she tried to eat it right now, it would be a fight between breathing and having an orgasm, and right then, she didn't know which one she preferred.

Roth angled her hips up, and suddenly he was hitting a spot inside of her that made her no longer think about her stomach.

"Oh fuck, right there, Roth," Lily groaned, her hand grabbing at something —anything—to brace herself.

"Oh, mother of all that is.... Fuck...."

Lily grunted, her head turning toward the voice that was not Roth's. Her eyes widened when she saw Ash standing in the dining room doorway. A squeal ripped from her throat at the same time she orgasmed, making it turn into a moan. She closed her eyes and lowered her head to the table as Roth hovered over her.

"Turn around," Roth ordered. It took her a second to realize he was talking to Ash. Good, because her legs were jelly, and if she had to do anything other than breathe, then she'd collapse.

"What the hell, man?" Ash whined. "Why can't you fuck in a bedroom like a normal person? I so didn't want that visual seared into my brain."

"If you value your life, you will unsear it," Roth threatened as he swiped a cloth between Lily's legs and helped her pull her clothing back on. The sound of a zipper told her he had finished righting his own clothing.

Lily sighed against the table, finally catching her breath. She inched up onto her elbows and then collapsed into the chair Roth had slid out for her. She winced as she sat down, the remnants of their lovemaking still throbbing between her legs.

Lifting her burning face to the back of Ash's head, she propped her head in her hand, trying to ignore what had just happened. "What are you doing here anyway?"

Ash shifted to peek over his shoulder. When he saw it was safe, Ash turned completely around with a grunt. "I didn't know I needed to announce my arrival, or I would have." He eyeballed the two of them. "When did you two start—?"

"That's none of your concern," Roth interrupted him with a dark look. "Give me your report."

Keeping her attention on Ash, she listened to him explain how he finally found a way into Utopia and what went down there. Lily was only half listening because her eyes had found that plate of bread once more. Except this time, she was too tired and sore to reach out and grab it.

Roth reached across the table and picked the plate up, placing it in front of her.

God, she loved that man.

She stuffed her face while Ash talked about evading the sentries and hiding out in the woods.

"Did you know they have two suns?" He held up two fingers. "Two! Like they need more than one." Ash threw his hands up in the air and then scratched the back of his head as he glared down at the ground. "Then that asshole archangel had to get in the middle of everything. Like I couldn't save my own mate."

"Archangel?" Lily asked through a mouthful of bread. "Which one?"

Ash crossed his arms over his chest and scowled. "Michael."

Lily choked on the bread. Coughing, she thumped her chest, trying to dislodge the food from her esophagus. Gasping for breath, Lily grabbed the cup Roth held out to her and chugged its contents. "You mean Raven's dad was there? He stopped you? Why?"

Roth leaned against the table next to her and smirked. "Michael probably knew you would get caught as you did."

Snapping to attention, Ash stalked across the room to scowl at Roth. "I had it all under control. It's not my fault the place was guarded up to its tits. You'd think, with it being Utopia, it wouldn't be so worried about trespassers."

Lily slammed her cup down on the table. "What about Raven? Did you save her?" She pushed to her feet and searched the room. "Obviously she's not with you."

"Well, obviously not." Ash glared at her. "Or she would be here."

Lily huffed. "Don't leave us in suspense here, Ash. I feel guilty enough waiting around here while she's being tortured. Don't make me beg."

Roth rubbed her back with a soft expression. "You were training. You can't save her if you can't protect yourself." She leaned her head against his shoulder, allowing him to comfort her.

"How do you think I feel?" Ash snarled. "I couldn't even save her. Her daddy did." He muttered a few choice words about Michael under his breath that Lily was sure were blasphemous, but she didn't think a hellhound worried about that kind of thing.

Lily arched her brows. "So... Raven is with Michael?"

Ash's expression turned morose. "Yes."

Roth chuckled. "For someone whose

mate has been saved, you do not sound pleased."

Pouting, Ash scuffed his shoe on the floor, muttering under his breath, "I wanted to be the one to save her."

Eyes rolling up at the immaturity of men, Lily asked, "Isn't Raven's safety more important?"

"Of course it is."

"Then maybe"—Lily moved away from Roth and shoved a finger at Ash's chest —"you stop acting like a big baby and be happy that she's safe with her dad."

"But I—"

Roth interrupted Ash, "I believe Lily is correct. The important thing is she is safe, and we can focus on the more pressing matters at hand."

Smoke curled out of the hellhound's nostrils before Ash finally sighed in defeat. "Fine. But I don't like it."

"No one said you had to." Roth patted his friend on the shoulder. "Now that you are back, I could use your help."

"Oh yeah?" Ash eyed Roth with interest. "With what?"

"Training Lily to take the throne, of course." Roth gestured to Lily. "We were about due for a bigger challenge. Don't you think, my love?"

Lily grimaced. "Oh, yeah. Sure."

Great, more work. And on top of that,

no more sex at dinner or in the library or on the training fields. Lily forced a smile at Ash, who seemed happier now that he had a task. At least there was that.

Gabriel

"What do you mean, she got away?" Gabriel snarled at the quivering angel before him. Bugs, all of them. Useless cretins not even worth the holy ground they walked on.

The angel rubbed his hands together and stared down at the ground, a tic forming on the side of his face as his voice shook. "That is...your greatness... we don't know how... but... but somehow she wasn't in her room at rounds check."

Gabriel rubbed a hand down his face and scowled. "I know what you meant. I mean how!" He gestured wildly around the room, stalking back and forth across the bloodied floor where his only hope to locate the heir had once been chained. "How did someone waltz in without anyone noticing them and take my most prized possession?" He stopped in front of the angel, towering over him. "Where were the guards?"

"Uh... uh.... Well, you see...." His eyes darted from side to side, clearly not wanting to tell Gabriel what happened. "There was an intruder out on the emerald plains, and most of the sentries were trying to track it down... so there weren't as many guards—"

"Enough!" Gabriel snapped, gnashing his teeth together as he spun around and glared at the broken chains. The chains were snapped at the lock, and a large chunk of stone had been ripped from the wall along with the bolted metal. His gaze dropped suspiciously to one cuff that had been left unbroken.

Could the Nephilim have escaped on her own? It wasn't impossible. It would not take much to break one's own hand and slip the bonds. Though, Gabriel had thought he had worn her down enough that the thought of even trying to escape would have been laughable.

Apparently not.

Still, the way the chains had been torn from the wall without concern for the possibility of being heard did not read like someone trying to make a stealthy escape. No, it read like someone arrogant and unbothered by the thought of being caught.

For a brief moment, Gabriel wondered if the Nephilim's father had played a part in her escape.

Shaking his head, Gabriel smirked. No. Michael didn't care for his children any more than Gabriel cared for any of the brats he'd sired. They were mistakes that should have been wiped out the moment they were conceived.

Regardless of who helped her, Gabriel would now have to escalate his plan. If he couldn't find the heir and take her down before she took over Hell, then he would just have to destroy Hell itself.

His lip curved up as Gabriel turned back to the groveling angel. "Call all the angels back from Earth. We have work to do." Gabriel shoved past the angel and into the hallway, the cretin scrambling after him as he went.

"What... what do you plan to do?" the sniveling fool asked.

Gabriel stopped in his tracks, his gaze hitting the horizon. "We're going to war."

Raven

"No training today?" Michael asked, standing in the doorway of her bedroom.

Raven turned from her window and shook her head in response to her father. "No. Not today. I thought I might take a walk."

Michael's face pinched together, but he didn't say anything.

"What?" Raven didn't try to hide the exasperation in her voice. "I've been cooped up in this place for weeks now. I need to get out. See the suns again."

Clearing his throat, Michael shoved his hands into his pockets and inclined his head. "I understand. I know you are anxious to get moving. To get back to that..." Michael visibly swallowed as if it hurt to speak. "Hellhound."

"He has a name," Raven quipped, narrowing her eyes.

"Oh, yes. Ash, was it?" Michael's mouth flattened into a thin line. "I'm not sure you should rely on a hellhound to keep you safe."

Raven stood abruptly to her feet, stalking across the room to stand before her father. "I don't count on anyone but me to keep me safe. And I'd take that hellhound you so blatantly object to at my back any day over a self-absorbed holier-than-thou archangel." She shoved a finger into his chest with a harrumph before pushing past him and out the door.

She didn't know where she was going exactly. Raven just knew she couldn't stay there for one more minute.

Her boots stomped along the hallway, making satisfying thuds with each hit. Raven hoped it cracked Michael's perfect tile in his perfect house of his goddamn perfect life. How dare he talk shit about her mate! Where did Michael get off trying to run her life? He wasn't there for the first few centuries. Why should he bother now?

Sure, he had saved her from Gabriel, taken her into his home, hidden her away like some fugitive he harbored.... Raven slowed to a stop before the front door, frowning back the way she came.

Michael had gone above and beyond to show he cared. Could she really fault him for trying to be the father she always wanted?

Raven shook her head to clear her roaring emotions. She just needed some fresh air. That was it. Then she would come back and talk to Michael like a rational adult and not some defiant child.

Pulling open the door, Raven stepped out of the house and onto the paved road. Then she started walking, not caring where she was headed.

Why the angels bothered to pave anything since everyone could fly, she'd never know. Perhaps it was an aesthetic thing. Regardless, it made Raven long for the plains' emerald green, which waited just outside the gates of Utopia's main center.

How long had it been since she'd run through those fields, barefooted with her wings spread wide? It had to be at least a decade or two. She'd let her life get so wrapped up in finding the heir that she had forgotten to live.

Well, with Lily found, she'd just have to change that.

Thinking of her friend made her sigh. She wondered how Lily and the others were doing. If they were thinking of her. If they knew she was all right. Raven didn't fault them for not coming for her.

Lily had more important things to worry about than a single Nephilim. At least Ash came for her.

Raven smiled a secret grin to herself, pulling her lower lip in between her teeth as she thought of the hellhound. How had she ever hated him? There was so much about him that she had turned her nose up at, but now she'd give anything to see him.

The stupid way he styled his hair so it flipped up to the side. The chinos he always seemed to wear. The way his voice would dip into a low growl when they argued. The fire in those green eyes sent thrills to her girly parts every time they landed on her.

"Hey, watch it."

Her head jerked up at the voice. "Oh, sorry." She sidestepped the group of angels in full golden armor, their wings out behind them as they marched through the streets.

Strange.

Raven stared after the angels as they turned down a pathway. Where were they going? No one wore full armor unless they were on duty, and Raven had never seen the streets so full of soldiers before. Not thinking twice about her actions, Raven glanced around her before nonchalantly heading in the same direction as them.

Forcing herself not to hurry after the parade of angels, Raven took on the guise of a shopper, stopping at one booth or the next without ever buying anything. She ducked behind a cart of vases as the troop stopped suddenly, their commander yelling, "Halt."

After a moment or two, the commander shouted, "Proceed." Then they were on the move again. Raven waited a few minutes before hustling out from behind the cart, gaining her several curious looks from working angels near her. She didn't pay them any mind, her attention set on the group ahead of her.

A sinking feeling set in her stomach as they turned down another street and moved toward a sickeningly familiar building. Gabriel's place. She had always meant to come back here eventually to take her revenge or burn it to the ground. However, seeing it now only made her insides twist into knots.

Raven continued down the path after taking a few deep breaths until she came to a stop before the entryway wall, her back pressed to the freezing stone. Her ears strained to listen to what was being said.

"What are you, a demon? Do you call that a line? I've seen hellhounds with cleaner jowls than that armor. I should be able to see my face in it, do you understand?" The commander paused and then yelled, "I said, do you understand me, angel?"

"Yes, Commander. Right away, Commander." The angel in question must have moved because the commander was screaming at him again, "Not now, you moron. Gabriel will be here any minute. Do you want to make us all look like fools?"

"Yes, Commander. I mean, no, Commander."

"Just go get back in place." The commander sighed heavily and muttered under his breath something Raven couldn't catch.

With everything quiet, Raven took the chance to peer around the corner. She'd been lucky that the angels were all so concerned about what was going on inside the gates and not the Nephilim loitering outside the gates. Hopefully, no one remembered Raven from her time there.

"Attention!" someone called out, and every angel's back went ramrod straight, their wings tucked in behind them. Raven's eyes narrowed until she caught sight of the blond-haired asshole striding through the courtyard as if he had all the time in the world.

Raven let her eyes linger on him, a boiling rage building inside of her. All it would take was one well-placed cut to bring the bastard to his knees.

"Report, Commander," Gabriel's arrogant voice boomed out, knocking her out of her fantasy.

Eyes widening, Raven realized she had stepped out of the shadows in her bloodlust and was practically gawking at the group. Thankfully, none of them were paying any mind to what was behind them with the archangel surveying them. Raven slipped back behind the wall again, her breath coming out in short, fast pants.

Placing a hand to her chest, she willed her heart to slow.

That had been a close one.

Swallowing, Raven leaned toward the entrance once more, listening to the commander's words.

"We have five thousand lower-level Nephilim. Fourteen hundred angels. All battle-ready and awaiting your orders, your greatness."

"Wonderful," Gabriel said.

Raven didn't need to see his face to know he would be grinning from ear to ear. She'd spent enough time with him to recognize when he was pleased with himself. Somehow, having her eyes closed while being tortured helped. Raven hadn't needed to see Gabriel's infuriating face. However, it had made her ears all too aware of his patronizing voice.

"I want everyone to be prepared to march on Hell in the next twenty-four hours. I don't want to give those filthy demons a chance to find out what we are doing."

"But your greatness," the commander began, "how will they know?" His voice was cut off by a gurgling sound.

Raven, tempted to see once more, leaned toward the edge in time to see Gabriel's hand come around the commander's throat. Gabriel lifted the angel off the ground and brought him close to his face.

"Because I am not stupid enough to think there are not demon sympathizers here in Utopia." He dropped the commander unceremoniously back to the ground and turned away, his wings kicking out behind him. "I have work to do. Be ready."

Raven jerked back against the wall, her heart racing as Gabriel took to the sky.

They were going to attack Hell! She had to warn Ash. They needed to be ready. She could no longer wait here in Utopia for the time to come. The time was now.

Resolve on her face, Raven pivoted on her heel and nearly walked into someone. "Oh, I'm sorry," she muttered without looking up.

"Don't be."

Horror filled Raven. She lifted her head slowly to meet the gaze of her worst nightmare and sworn enemy.

Gabriel beamed at her. "I'm not."

Raven's dark wings unfurled behind her. Instantly, several sets of hands latched on to her wings and body. She struggled against soldiers, who had appeared out of nowhere, determined to not be captured again.

Gabriel laughed with glee. "Fighting it is futile. You should have always known you'd be back and at my mercy."

Kicking out, Raven tried to at least get the bastard in his smirking face. Her attempt only made him laugh harder. Held back, Raven could only glare at Gabriel as he strolled toward her. He grabbed her chin and stroked a finger along her cheek.

"Sadly, as much as I'd love to play with you again, I have other pressing matters at hand."

Raven spit at him. "Go to Hell."

"Oh, dear sweet angel, I plan to." Gabriel's sinister grin would haunt her for the rest of her life. No matter how long that might be.

"This time, I won't make the mistake of putting you somewhere easy to find,"

Gabriel continued as he strolled ahead of her down a long and dark corridor. They weren't at his house anymore. In fact, Raven had no idea where they were. This was a part of Utopia she'd never been before.

"You won't get away with this," Raven spat at Gabriel's back. "Lily will stop you."

Gabriel raised a brow at her over his shoulder. "Lily, is it? Good to know. I like to know who I'm slaughtering when the time comes. It makes it all so much more personal, don't you think, Raven dear?"

Raven snarled in response.

They walked for a little longer, going down a set of stairs, each step sounding Raven's fate. The air grew cold, and she shivered. She had never been cold in Utopia. She didn't think it was possible. And yet it was. Goosebumps pebbled her skin, and she jerked at the hands on her once more. It didn't accomplish anything but getting her thrown into the wall, scraping the side of her face against the freezing stone.

Once they reached the bottom, the light seemed to die. There was enough to see the next couple of feet in front of her, then nothing but darkness. She didn't even see the door to her cell until they were right upon it.

"Welcome to your new home." Gabriel bowed mockingly as a soldier opened the wooden door for her. "I hope you find it to your liking."

The soldiers holding her at sword-point gave her a little encouragement with the sharp ends at her back. Scowling, Raven shuffled into the pitch-dark room. Even the scant light from the hallway did nothing to illuminate it. There could have been several others in that room for all she knew, which kept her firmly planted where she stood.

"Don't get too lonely without me," Gabriel crooned before shutting the door in her face.

Raven waited a few moments until the footsteps were far enough away, and then she raced back the way she came. Falling against the door, Raven groped around until she found the handle. Locked. Of course it was. Why would she possibly think otherwise? Foolish wishful thinking.

Scowling at herself, Raven stepped back from the door, arms crossed and one foot tapping. A thought occurred to her. Turning on her heel, she walked back several paces before spinning around and running full force at the door.

Pain radiated up her shoulder, and she sank to the ground with a whimper. The door mocked her as she leaned against it. *Damn it.*

Sighing, Raven pulled her knees up to her chest and stared into the darkness of the room. Her eyes had adjusted slightly. Still, the room was nothing but black on top of black. Narrowing her eyes, she hesitantly called out, "Hello?"

When nothing answered her, Raven inched back to her feet. Placing her hand on the door, she used it as a guide to find the wall and then worked her way around the room. It wasn't a large room. She had managed to get around the entire thing within a few seconds, only once bumping into what was probably a bucket. Nothing else filled the room. Nothing useful.

Sinking to the ground against the door once more, Raven contemplated the pickle she had gotten herself into this time. No one knew where she was, and even her father wouldn't come for her this time, Raven was sure of it. No doubt he thought she'd run off after their fight. And with Ash thinking she was safe with her father, he wouldn't be worried about finding her. Not until it was too late, and Gabriel's army had destroyed them all.

That thought made Raven jump back onto her feet.

No. She would not sit idly by while her friends died at that asshole's hands.

Raven scoured her body for what she had. Luckily, Gabriel had been too busy gloating to search her before he left. Unluckily, she hadn't grabbed anything useful she could use. She sighed and dragged a hand through her hair.

"Ow!" Raven's hand caught on something. Oh. Oh. A bobby pin! Yes. She had bothered to do her hair this morning. Thank God for little favors.

Carefully extracting the pin from her hair, she bent it slightly until it was open enough to get into the keyhole.

Given Raven was not an expert lock picker—in fact, she had only ever tried once or twice—the likelihood of this actually working was lower than low. It was so low that Raven didn't dare to hope. Still, she worked on the lock until her head hurt and her hands shook. Then finally, just when she was about to give up, there was a click. The door swung open. Freedom waited just beyond the darkness, and Raven wasn't wasting any time.

Rushing out the door, Raven scanned the dark hallway and considered which way to go. Up the stairs was the exit, and down the hallway led.... Raven didn't even want to think about going into even more darkness.

Sprinting to the stairs, Raven took them two at a time until she reached the next level's platform. This had been the way they had come; Raven was sure of it.

Except voices were coming from the direction she needed to go, and they were headed right for her.

Raven darted up the next set of stairs and the next. Maybe she could reach the roof and fly out of there. Then she could quickly figure out where she was at and get back to her father's house.

Her plan formed, Raven set forth, one staircase after another, until her legs burned in complaint. She pushed through the pain, her lungs clenching from the effort. When she finally reached the top, Raven could have kissed the ground had it not been for the doorway before her.

Unlike anything she had ever seen, the door was made of some kind of glass or crystal. It gleamed from the light outside the narrow window, making Raven wince. Not to be distracted by its beauty, Raven went over to the window and peered out.

A white castle spread out beneath her, nothing like any of the others in Utopia. In fact, Raven didn't remember ever seeing this particular castle... ever. Frowning as she pulled away from the window, Raven moved back over to the door.

It wouldn't hurt just to take a peek, right? It could be the exit. No harm in looking.

There was no door handle on the crystal entrance, so Raven pressed her hands against the surface of the door and pushed. Expecting it to stay where it was, Raven let out a little scream when the door easily swung open. Falling onto her hands and knees, she winced before jerking her head up and searching for danger.

What she found was a long gleaming white throne room. Large crystal pillars spanned from the floor to the piercing white ceiling. Across the throne room sat a throne of white and gold. There was someone on that throne, and they were staring right at her.

Raven

Scrambling to her feet, Raven spun around to leave the way she came when a voice smooth as silk voice called out, "Don't leave. I never get any visitors. Please come forward."

Torn between survival and curiosity, Raven steeled her back and twisted back around. She made the long trek across the room to the throne where the most beautiful man she had ever seen sat playing a game of solitaire.

Long golden hair fell over broad shoulders, and piercing blue eyes flicked from the cards before him and up to her before back again. His soft jawline made him almost seem effeminate and the muscular body beneath the white shirt and slacks was apparent.

"Uh, hi." Raven grimaced as her voice came out in a squeak.

Before her, the man didn't seem to notice as he placed a queen of hearts on top of a king of spades. "I can assume you aren't here of your own volition, so I'll be grateful for the company for as long as you can spare it. Though, I do assume your jailers will be here soon."

Holding back a scowl, Raven forced herself not to think of the archangel responsible for her current predicament. "Yeah, I probably shouldn't linger here." She glanced around the throne room once more. "Wherever here is," she muttered more to herself than to him.

"It's a laughable excuse for a jail cell," the man responded to her unintentional question. "Meant to mock me. Still, I quite like it." He leaned back from his cards and crossed one long leg over the other. "What is your name, Nephilim?"

Raven swallowed back a gasp. He must be strong if he could tell what she was so easily. Not wanting to offend him, she answered, "Raven. My name is Raven."

The beautiful man's gaze skimmed over her face and then down her body. Raven flushed with embarrassment at his honest assessment. "You are a daughter of Michael, are you not?"

Gaping at him, Raven stuttered out, "How did you know that?"

He gestured a slender hand in her

direction. "You have your father's chin, and I'd know those eyes anywhere." A small smile played on his full lips. Had Ash not been the one for her, Raven would have easily fallen for this man. Even if he was imprisoned.

"You know my father?" Raven prompted, not sure how much she could ask without being reprimanded. The man definitely smelled of upper celestial power. Perhaps an archangel. Thinking better of it, she decided not. No archangel would let themselves be trapped here.

The man picked up a card, the jack of diamonds. "We've known each other for what seems like forever. It's hard to remember a time when we didn't know each other. I—"

The crystal door Raven had entered burst open, and half a dozen guards poured in. "There she is! Get her." *Uh-oh. Time's up.*

Before Raven could get two steps, the guards were upon her. Gabriel must really want to keep her if he sent that many men after her, especially when he had a war to wage.

She struggled against the guards, kicking and biting, even going so far as to pull hair, anything to get away from them. She would not go back into that darkness. There was so much more for her to do, of her life to live, and Gabriel was not going to take one more second of it away from her.

"Excuse me," the man called out, and all the guards stopped what they were doing, staring at him in horror. He stood from his throne and adjusted the cuffs of his sleeves before he disappeared in an instant. Reappearing behind one of the guards, he slashed his hand, the long nails on his fingers slicing through the guard's neck. Blood spurted from his neck, hitting Raven's shoes.

A few guards scrambled to get away from him only to be cut down before they made it more than a few steps away. Some of the guards had more resolve, holding on to her like she was their ticket to the chocolate factory. When the man had cut down every single one of their friends, their grip on her loosened, and they now had to decide if she was really worth dying over.

Raven knew what she voted for.

"Please, don't," one of the guards begged, holding his hands up and backing away from him. "We were only doing our job."

The man grimaced, the guards whimpering, and then disappeared once more. He materialized behind the guard and broke his neck with a crack, cutting off the horrible keening sound at the source.

One final guard remained, and he

pulled a sword from his waist, prepared to fight over her. If the guard wasn't trying to keep her locked up, she might have rooted for him against this terrifying stranger. Yet, the thought of going back to the black abyss down below made her hope the stranger ripped the guard's head off.

Even threatened with a weapon when he had none, the man's expression never changed. If anything, he looked impatient to finish the confrontation.

The guard charged the stranger with a loud yell, lashing out with his sword in a wide arc. The sword's metal hit the white tile with a sonorous clang as the man sidestepped his attack. He jerked his knee up. The guard groaned. He didn't have time to clutch his stomach before the stranger shoved an elbow into his back. The guard let out a high-pitched squeal as something broke. Then the man spun around and kicked the guard across the room. The guard smashed into the nearby column and crumbled onto the ground, no longer moving or making a sound.

With all the guards taken care of, the beautiful man brushed his hands off and sniffed. "It is rude to interrupt someone when they are talking." He stepped on the back of one of the guards as he made his way back to the throne.

Raven clutched her arms around herself, staring down at the fallen guards. Not one of them twitched or moved. He'd been so fast. She'd barely seen him move. How? How did he move like that?

"Tell me, Raven."

Swallowing her fear, Raven glanced back to the man on the throne. He leaned his face against his fist and peered back at her, almost bored. "Why would these guards touch a daughter of Michael?"

"Uhh...." Raven struggled to find her words, still dumbfounded by what had just happened. "It's a long story."

Smiling, the man waved his hand around the room. "I'm not going anywhere. I think we have time." He offered her a seat on the chair off to the side.

In all honesty, Raven didn't have time to linger around this man, whoever he may be. She needed to get to Hell and warn Lily and the others of Gabriel's plans. However, the six dead guards littering the ground made her hesitant to refuse him.

Scrunching up her nose at the bodies around her, Raven carefully stepped over one and then another body. Her foot kicked one of the guards in the head. "Oops, sorry."

Raven reached the front of the room and took the offered seat next to him. She shifted in her chair, not sure what to do next.

"Drink?" the man prompted, picking up a wine glass on the table beside him.

Finding herself parched, Raven nodded once. "Sure. I mean, yes. Thank you."

"Please," he chuckled, pouring dark red liquid from a pitcher into each glass. "Relax. If I wanted to kill you, you'd be dead."

Surprisingly, that wasn't comforting.

"Besides," he offered her one of the glasses, "I am quite fond of your father. I wouldn't want to cause him any grief. Especially that of losing a daughter."

Raven wrapped her fingers around the glass, staring at the man. A sort of sadness had come over him that she didn't understand. It made her, despite her fear, want to console him. Then, as sudden as the emotion had appeared on his face, it was gone. A small smile crept over his face.

"So, you were telling me why anyone would dare touch you. I'm sure your father is quite worried about you. Does he know that you are here?"

Sipping from her glass, Raven swallowed as she shook her head. "I doubt it." She paused and lowered the glass to her lap, staring off at the empty walls. "We had a fight, and I ran out of the house. He likely thinks I'm just off having a tantrum."

"Ah," the man hummed, twirling his own wine glass around in between his fingers. "I'm sure he will come looking for you shortly. A father never forgets his daughter, no matter how much pain they cause them."

There it was again—that sadness. Raven stared at the man for a long moment, trying to make sense of him. What was a gorgeous and yet powerful creature such as himself doing locked up? It was clear he could have left at any time. Why hadn't he? Then there was how he kept talking about children as if he had one of his own and regretted... something. What was it?

"Is there something on my face?" The man touched along his mouth and chin, searching for the nonexistent thing. That was when it clicked.

The piercing blue eyes. The mouth. The chin. She had seen them somewhere else before, on someone before. In fact, if she threw violet hair on the man, he would look almost exactly like....

Raven jumped to her feet, her wine glass falling from slack fingers to shatter on the ground. Gaping at the man, she pointed a finger at him. "You're... you're Lucifer!"

Only vaguely paying any mind to the

mess Raven had made, the man stared up at her and grinned a devious smile. "In the flesh."

Lucifer

The child standing before him gaped. She looked so much like her father it was laughable to think anyone would mistake her for the daughter of anyone else. It was apparent as soon as one saw Michael's expression on his progeny's face.

When Raven had walked into his prison, Lucifer had thought it may have been a ploy by his brother Gabriel to get him to tell him where the Wicked Crown was. Then when the girl didn't even seem to know who he was, Lucifer had taken a closer look.

Why had Michael allowed Gabriel to capture his only daughter? Didn't he know how precious they were? Lucifer had lost his child; he did not want to see his brother do the same.

"Gabriel must want something from you quite badly if he is sending guards to take you from here," Lucifer commented to the still stunned Nephilim. He supposed he should have introduced himself when she first appeared. However, it was much more entertaining to let her flounder a bit. You never knew what someone would say when they didn't know who they were talking to. It was much easier than trying to torture it out of them. And far more amusing when you were imprisoned forever.

"Well, yes," Raven paused, pulling her lower lip between her teeth. "He's about to wage war on Hell."

Lucifer arched a brow. "Why would he bother with that place? There's nothing there of interest to him." He leaned back on his throne and held his arms out to his sides. "He has me. What else could he want?"

Raven frowned, her brows scrunching together. "You... you don't know, do you?"

"Know what, my dear?"

She took a step toward him and then opened her mouth. Raven clamped it shut. She opened her mouth again and lifted a finger. Sighing, Raven dropped her arms to her side and gave him a curious look that seemed like... pity? Did she pity him? Why?

"I don't know how to tell you this. In fact, it shouldn't be me telling you this at all." Raven paced in front of him, wringing her hands as she spoke. "You should have been the one to find her. You shouldn't have been locked away here while the whole world searched for the one thing you want more than anything in the world." She huffed a laugh and tugged on a lock of the white-blonde bob of her hair. "Who could have known that it would be me who would be the one to stand before the great Lucifer and tell him that..." Her eyes shone as she put both hands on her cheeks and said, "...his daughter is alive and well."

The bemusement Lucifer had been feeling evaporated. His eyes narrowed on the child before him. "Did your father put you up to this? Is this some kind of sick and twisted joke?"

Raven shook her head vehemently. "No. No. It's not. She's in Hell right now. With Roth."

Lucifer stared at her for a moment longer, trying to process the information she had told him. His entire world imploded on itself as he realized his daughter was not being held captive. That his entire existence here as a prisoner in Utopia had been a ruse to keep him in line.

No more.

"Tell me everything."

Startled by his command, Raven took a step back from him. She licked her lips and took a deep breath. "Like I said, it's a long story. And I would love to tell it to you, but seeing as Gabriel is about to go destroy Hell to keep it from Lily, I think it might be best to save the explanations for later. Don't you think?"

As much as Lucifer wanted to know everything, he could sense the urgency in the girl. "Very well. Let's go." Lucifer stood and strode across the room, the Nephilim following close behind him.

White wings burst from Lucifer's back. As he beat them behind him, he pushed off the ground and shot into the sky. Faster than a shooting star, Lucifer crashed through the ceiling, proving the prison they thought would keep him was laughable at best. He briefly glanced down to make sure Raven was following after him. She flew behind him, her eyes wide as her wings flapped to keep up.

An alarm sounded off in the distance. Lucifer snorted. *Idiots. Let's see them try and stop me.*

They flew over the castle that had been his prison for the last millennium. He didn't bother to stop and admire the world around him. He didn't care if he ever saw Utopia again. The only thing he wanted to see right now was his daughter's beautiful smiling face. Nothing and no one was going to stop him.

A host of lower-level angels soared up beneath them, their swords out and their golden armor gleaming. There were other colors in the universe. Why didn't they mix it up sometime? Maybe a bit of red here. A splash of purple. There were better colors than gold out there. He might be the morning star, but even he had his limits.

"Lucifer...," Raven called out behind him, worry in her voice.

Smirking at the oncoming siege, Lucifer's wings closed around him as he twisted into a nosedive into the middle of the fray. His wings flared open around him, knocking back several angels. Fire burst from his palms, and he spun around like a cyclone, sucking up the nearby angels. They burned as they were ripped apart, thrown from his whirlwind of fire. Before he could gloat at the ease of their deaths, another fifty angels were upon him.

"This is going to get old." Lucifer scowled. Barreling into one of the angels, he took his sword and his neighbor's. Not wanting to waste any more magic on these vermin, Lucifer speared through the lot of them, slashing as he went. He aimed for their wings rather than the kill. He didn't have time to worry about killing each and every one of them. If they couldn't fly, they couldn't get in his way.

Once he had cut a pathway through them, he yelled back at Raven, "Come. Quickly."

He didn't wait to see if she would follow, his focus on getting past the outer ring of the palace. Once they hit that, they wouldn't encounter much resistance, and then they could get to the portal just beyond the gate.

When they were just at the edge of the palace, a dark figure swooped up into the sky. Lucifer pulled up short and narrowed his gaze. Long white hair flowed down to the angel's ankles, his wings a gray color as they flapped behind him. The arrogance on the angel's face was only solidified by the lack of armor on his body. The only protection he bothered with were two pauldrons, and even those weren't much protection.

"Raphael. They still have you on guard duty?" Lucifer taunted with a grin.

"Lucifer," a low timbre of a voice called out. "I was wondering when you would try to break out of your cage."

Lucifer snorted. "Try?" He held his

arms out to the sides. "It looks like I have succeeded."

The other archangel unsheathed his sword and swiped it to the side. "Not yet, you haven't."

Tightening his grip on his own weapons, Lucifer prepared to charge. Fighting Raphael would not be like fighting the hordes of low-level angels. Where they were slow, he was fast. Where they were weak, he was strong.

Raphael would not be either.

Their swords clashed together, putting them a hair's breadth away from each other. Their wings flapped vigorously, each trying to knock through the other's defenses.

"What's your rush, Lucifer?" Raphael taunted, his eyes twinkling with malice.

Lucifer growled, putting all his strength into his swordplay. "I'm going to get my daughter."

"Oh, you mean the one Gabriel is about to destroy?" Raphael shoved Lucifer back. "You are wasting your time. Just go back to your cage like a good little devil."

Sneering at the name, Lucifer flipped them around in the air until they broke apart. "Don't tell me you're still sore that the humans know me, but not a lowly soldier."

Raphael straightened to his full

height and snarled, "I am not a lowly soldier. I am a general, and I demand the respect I am owed."

Lucifer laughed. "No one will respect a general the way they respect a king." He gestured to himself with the hilt of his sword. "You simply cannot compete."

"You are not a king!" Raphael charged at him, sword at the ready.

That's it, Raphael. Get riled up. Let your anger make you sloppy.

Lucifer parried every swipe and hit, growing more confident that he had gotten under Raphael's skin. "Admit it, Raph. You'll never be as good as me."

The other archangel jumped back and lifted a hand, shooting beams of light out of his palm. Lucifer dodged and swerved. When Raphael had finally exhausted his magical barrage, Lucifer threw his head back and laughed. "Is that all you've got?"

He needed Raphael to tire out. Lucifer might act as if he were all-powerful, but he was beginning to feel drained from all the angels he'd fought. He needed a breather, and if he could get Raphael to a weaker form, it would be much easier on himself to get past him.

"I despise you!" Raphael shouted, swinging his sword wildly. "You are not fit to be called an angel—even a fallen one.

You have made the rest of us a laughing-stock. Why won't you die?"

Barely able to keep up with Raphael's attacks, Lucifer couldn't get a word out to respond. He had to focus on the fight and stop picking on the archangel, or he'd find himself on the wrong end of Raphael's sword.

Pain sliced through his left wing as he missed one of Raphael's attacks. Lucifer schooled his face so he did not show it. The moment Raphael found a weakness, it would all be over. He had to end this quickly.

"What, the great King of Hell at a loss for words?" Raphael sneered, locking his sword with Lucifer's.

Forcing a smile to his face, Lucifer cocked his head to one side. "No. Just tired of talking to such a weakling." He used his words as a distraction as he dropped one sword between them.

"Who are you calling—"

Raphael's words were cut off by a grunt as Lucifer's sword pierced through his gut and out the back. Blood spurted from Raphael's mouth, and his eyes went wide. Lucifer released the blade and pushed back, letting Raphael fall to the ground all on his own.

"Wow, that was... wow." Raven cried out, appearing beside him. "I've never seen a fight like that before. You were incredible."

Lucifer allowed himself to wince. "Yes. Well, we are wasting time."

"Oh, yeah. Let's go." Raven took off in front of him, and Lucifer took the chance to look at his wing. Blood seeped from the wound, and the pain was almost blinding. Pushing through the hurt, Lucifer raced after her. They made it past the outer ring of the palace without encountering anyone else. Lucifer sighed as they began to descend.

A few feet from the ground, Lucifer collapsed before the swirling air. Everything hurt. Especially, his wings. He flexed them and pain radiated through his injured left wing.

"Are you going to be okay?" Raven asked, landing at his side.

Waving off her offered hand, Lucifer pushed up to his knees. "Yes. Give me a moment. I've had worse injuries than this." Lucifer struggled to get up, his legs buckling beneath him as he tried to stand. Raven caught him around the waist, helping him to his feet. "I won't be able to fly for a few minutes so it will be up to you to get us past the guards on the other side."

Raven's grip on him tightened, her face set in determination. "I've got you. I promise."

Lucifer placed a hand on her shoulder and smiled down at her. "I'm glad my daughter had a friend like you at her side. Her mother would have loved you too."

A flush crept over Raven's cheeks, and she ducked her head. "Thank you. Now, let's get you back to Hell."

Gabriel

Sitting at the dinner table, Gabriel mulled over how well everything was going for him. He might not have found the heir, but he would soon have all of Hell on their knees. Then there was the matter of the little angel who had gotten away.

It was exceptionally fortuitous that she had fallen into his lap. Gabriel was almost giddy at the thought of playing with her again. This time he didn't have to hold back because there was nothing that she had to offer him. No, Gabriel could play with her as he liked, and perhaps when he was done, he'd send her back to Michael in pieces. That would teach him to step out of line.

Humming to himself, Gabriel lifted his teacup to his lips and took a long drink. Soon. Soon everything would be as it should be. Lucifer in his prison. Hell in ruins. And Gabriel would have the highest honor of them all. He would be the one who finally took down Hell and with it, the heir.

Though, Gabriel would have liked to have the heir's head on a platter. It would have made an excellent dinner conversation piece. Sadly, they couldn't all get what they wanted. Gabriel would just have to be satisfied with the complete and utter destruction of everything she held dear.

There was a knock on the door. Quite pleased with himself, Gabriel didn't even feel annoyed at being interrupted at mealtime.

"Yes, come in already." Gabriel stared out the nearby window, the sky dimming and the stars coming out.

A shadow fell over him.

When they didn't speak, the first hint of annoyance pinched Gabriel's face. "Well? What is it?"

"There's news, your greatness."

Gabriel's mood picked up as he shifted around to face the informant. "News? Of the heir? Have they finally found her? Tell me quickly. I have much to prepare." Gabriel sat his cup down and began to think of all the ways he would maim and torture the beast of a child.

The informant shook his head and

quivered as he said, "No, your greatness. Not the heir."

Scoffing in irritation, Gabriel turned away from him. "Then I don't care. I have other things to do with my time than listening to some silly gossip." Gabriel picked his cup back up and began to count the stars as they pricked the sky.

"Even if it has to do with Lucifer?"

The cup in Gabriel's hand cracked and splintered beneath the pressure of his palm. Gabriel barely noticed the glass slicing into his flesh as he spun around on the informant. "What about Lucifer?"

The informant shook with fear, licking his lips as he continued, "He's escaped from his prison and has taken down quite a few of our guards, as well as Raphael, along the way."

"Raphael?" Gabriel shoved to his feet, his chair slamming to the ground with a loud thud. "We lost Raphael?"

"Well, he's not dead. Yet. Though he is gravely injured."

Gabriel grabbed the informant around the neck and lifted him in the air. "Tell me. Where is he? I will put him down myself once and for all."

The informant gasped through the hold Gabriel had on him. "He... left... through a... a portal."

Snarling, Gabriel threw the informant across the room, smiling when he hit the wall with a satisfying crack. Turning back to the dining room table, Gabriel pounded his fists on the surface. Why had Lucifer decided to break out now? They had been oh so careful the last millennium to make him think his child was still their captive. Could someone have told him? It was too much of a coincidence for them to not have. If he was going to Hell to fight, Gabriel had to make sure that he beat him there.

"Call the commander and tell them to be ready to move out now," Gabriel called out over his shoulder to the informant. The angel scrambled to his feet but didn't leave like Gabriel expected. "Well? What are you waiting for?"

"There's one more thing, your greatness."

Gabriel's fingers curled under the table's edges. "What. Is. It?"

"The Nephilim." The informant paused. "She was seen leaving... with Lucifer."

The table cracked beneath his palms as Gabriel lifted it and flung it on its side. He let out a rage-filled scream that had the informant running from the dining room. Gabriel would not lose. He would get them. The heir, Lucifer, and all of Hell would pay. They would all cower before the name of Gabriel and then suffer.

· · ·

Lily

Laying in Roth's arms was Lily's favorite place to be. Pressed up against his warm side, his hand stroking up and down her bare back, was better than anything Utopia could ever offer her.

It was even better when he had his wings out like he did now. They were soft and downy like a cloud and yet strong as steel. Lily just wanted to rub her whole body all over them, marking them as her own.

"What are you doing?" Roth asked, amusement in his voice as she wiggled a bit against his wings.

"Claiming you as mine," Lily declared, not even embarrassed by her actions.

Roth arched a brow and opened his eyes to peer down at her. "By marking my wings with your scent?"

Nodding enthusiastically, Lily wiggled her nude body just a bit more along the feathery edges. "Yep. I want everyone to know these are my wings."

A broad smile curved up Roth's handsome face. "And what of me? Do I get to mark your wings with my scent?"

Lily frowned. "I don't have any wings."

Roth stroked his fingers down her

back, circling around her upper muscles. "Not yet, but you will."

Flexing her back muscles, Lily tried to imagine what it would be like to have something sprouting there. It didn't seem possible. She'd always had her feet firmly planted on the ground, and the thought of having to learn to fly made her a bit nauseous.

"Don't worry," Roth murmured, cupping her face in his other hand. "Everyone must fall before they can fly. And I will be there to catch you every time."

Lily leaned over him, her nipples rubbing against his chest as she pressed her lips to his. She sighed into his mouth, their tongues caressing and intertwining. Lily would never get enough of this. If all she ever did for the rest of eternity was lay in Roth's arms, she would die a happy woman.

Something hard prodded her hip. She smiled into the kiss, her hand reaching down to wrap around the solid thickness of him. Roth made a low growl into her mouth.

"Treacherous woman."

Lily squeezed and moved her hand over him faster, enjoying the way she could make him lose control.

Roth grabbed her around the waist and picked her up, causing her to let out a squeal of delight, which morphed into a moan as she sank down on to his delicious hardness. Catching her breath, Lily locked eyes with Roth.

"Move for me, my mate."

Bracing her hands on his chest, Lily complied. Her hips lifted and sank back down in a tentative rhythm that matched their gasps and moans. They continued like that for a long while, just slowly making love to one another, neither in a hurry to get it over with. Then, as they crested over the edge together, Lily collapsed into Roth's arms, holding him tightly as if he might disappear.

Lily's heart raced and she licked her lips, opening her mouth to say something she had never said to anyone before. Never felt the absolute connection and need to express herself in such a way. If she thought too hard about it, she wouldn't do it. It terrified her to think he wouldn't say it back. That she was the only one who felt this way.

"I love you, Lily Star."

Her head jerked up at his words, her mouth agape. "How did you—"

Roth smiled softly at her. "How did I what?"

Smiling in return, Lily shook her head, pulling her lip between her teeth as she said, "I love you too."

"Good." Roth slapped her ass, causing

her to squeak and wiggle. "Otherwise, I would have to tie you to this bed until you did."

Lily giggled, coyly gazing up at him beneath her lashes. "Maybe you should, just to be sure."

Roth cupped her ass and drew her close. "Perhaps next time. We have training in the morning, and we both need to sleep."

Pouting, Lily gave in and snuggled in for the night. Yes, life in Hell was good.

Lily jerked awake, sitting up in bed.

Blinking her eyes, Lily tried to adjust them to the darkness of the room. She didn't know how long she had slept or what had woken her. Her gaze slipped over to Roth, whose even breathing told her he still slept on.

Lips tugging down at the edges, Lily slipped from the bed and padded across the room. She stepped into the bathroom and did her business. As Lily washed her hands, something tugged at her. She grabbed her chest like she would if she were in pain, and yet it wasn't exactly that. It was as if a string was attached to her heart, and something jerked on the other end.

Lily grabbed her robe and wrapped it

around her body, tying it tightly closed as she walked back into the bedroom. A glance at the bed showed her that Roth was indeed still asleep. A bit more than curious, Lily left the bedroom. She blinked at the light of the hallway, looking one way and then the other for some sign of life. No one was there—just her and that incessant tugging.

She let the urge to investigate overtake her as she walked down the hallway. A sinking feeling came over her as she left the wing of the palace where Roth and her room were located. Where was it taking her? Who was on the other end?

Her feet led her through the palace and down a familiar hallway. One that she had tried to avoid at all costs. Then she was standing before the black double doors. She hesitated at the threshold, not sure she should go in.

The last time she had gone in, the crown had almost taken her. Roth had warned her to stay away, and she had listened. Lily didn't want anyone to control her but herself, and the Wicked Crown was not likely to share control.

The incessant tugging pulled at her again until she doubled over and reached for the door. It opened far easier than last time. Like it was almost eager to have her inside. The pain in Lily's chest lessened with each step she took closer to the crown. Her heart pounded in her ears as the cool floor beneath her feet seemed to warm and pulsate. Hands reaching out, she could hear the whispering of the crown once more in her head.

Not that it had ever really gone away. It was always there in the back of Lily's mind, reminding her that it existed and was waiting for her. Now she could have it. The crown could be hers, as well as all the power that went with it. All she had to do was reach out and take it.

Her fingers were nearly brushing the crown when an alarm sounded. Like trumpets blaring in the sky, it pulled her from the tantalizing spell she had been under. Stumbling away from the crown, not taking the time to mull over what she had almost done, Lily scrambled from the room. When she hit the hallway, she ran into Bacchii.

"What's happening?" Lily asked, placing a hand on the succubus's arm to stop her.

Bacchii's eyes were wide, and fear etched across her face. "They're coming."

Roth

The sirens woke him from the dead of sleep. Roth's hand searched for Lily on her side of the bed. She wasn't there. Panic sliced through his chest as he launched himself into action.

Finding clothing was easy enough, though Roth had to remind himself that he would do Lily no good if he wasn't armed and ready to battle. The sirens blaring only meant one thing. The angels had come.

A knock on his door had him flying across the room, jerking it open while the servant still had a hand up. "Have you seen Lily?"

The servant, Travil, a lower-level demon who had earned his place at the palace after the fall of Lucifer, shook his head. "No, I have not, my prince." His bloodred hair was mussed over the small horns protruding from his head. His tail twitched nervously behind him. Even his scales seemed to twitch with worry.

Roth pushed past him, seeking his mate. Travil scrambled after him, still talking. "The lookouts have counted at least a thousand angels at the east edge of Purgatory."

"Who leads them?" Roth asked, sidestepping the servants and soldiers who scattered to get out of his way.

"Gabriel, my prince." Travil quieted, as if this was news to Roth. If anyone was going to make such a blatant attack on Hell, it would be that ego-inflated blowhard.

Stopping for a moment to drag a hand through his hair, Roth forced himself to calm. "How long do we have?"

Travil wrung his hands before him, not meeting his gaze.

"Travil." Roth grabbed the demon by the collar of his shirt. "We don't have all day. I need to know how long we have to gather our forces."

Swallowing hard, Travil winced. "Within the hour."

"Fuck." Roth dropped him and stalked forward once more. "Fuck. Fuck. Fuck." To Travil, he ordered, "Call everyone to arms. If they are on Earth, tell them to get back here now."

"But it might be too late by then, my prince."

"I don't care," Roth roared, causing everyone in the halls to pause. "Just do it. If Hell is going to fall, we aren't going to go down without a fight." He took a deep breath and then called out, "And someone, for the love of all things in Purgatory, find my mate!"

"She's with Bacchii, my prince." A single demon maid followed at his side. "I saw them heading toward the armory just a few moments ago."

Roth scowled. "Thank you."

Of course, his mate would already be up and in the middle of the chaos. Why would he think otherwise? Now, Roth was torn at what to do next. Find his mate or secure the palace, protecting those inside?

He could erect a shield around everyone, but without knowing how many angels there were out there, he had no idea how effective it would be, let alone how long he could hold it. There was also the problem that if he was shielding them, he couldn't do anything else, leaving Lily to take command alone. The protective side of him wanted nothing more than to make sure that she was safe and cared for. However, he had a duty to the demons, and if he didn't protect them, then there would be no one left to even think about protecting her.

Reluctantly, Roth turned away from the path that led to the armory and made for the palace's front. He needed to see how many were here already. Like Travil said, the likelihood that those on Earth were able to make it back in time was slim.

They had to try.

Roth would not go down in history as the prince of Hell who simply let the angels walk all over him. What would Lucifer think if he saw that? He would take his daughter back in a heartbeat, and Roth would not be able to forgive himself.

When he exited the palace, he could already tell they were going to be in trouble. Fewer than five hundred demons lined up in the front, most of whom had never seen a real battle in their lives. They hadn't had to face a conflict of this magnitude in a long time. Not since Lucifer himself was there. He had been so busy making sure that Lily could defend herself when the time came that he didn't think to make the rest of the palace prepare. Roth did not know how they would hold up against the legion of angels heading their way.

"Roth, there you are." Ash strode over to him, his body covered in the black-

and-red armor of his people. Leather covered his chest and legs, and Ash's forearms had metal strapped to them, the sigil of Hell embedded into each piece. The Wicked Crown. If only Lily were ready to take on such a powerful piece of weaponry, the angels coming after them wouldn't have a chance. Yet, Roth knew she wasn't prepared. He would rather them all die right there than let her be overtaken by the crown before she was strong enough to resist the evil temptation it presented. All that power was not suitable for one person, especially not one as good and pure as Lily Star.

"What do you have to report?" Roth asked, not bothering with pleasantries.

Unbothered by his abruptness, Ash answered, "We have four hundred and fifty-six demons from the palace and surrounding areas prepped and ready to fight. There are another two hundred on Earth that have been signaled to return. Though, I'm not sure how fast that will be."

"And the other rings?" Roth took a position at the front of the line, his eyes on the horizon. He couldn't see them yet, but he trusted Travil's word. If the angels would be here within the hour, they had to be ready.

Ash shook his head. "There are some who are coming, but the numbers are just too small. At this rate, the angels will be here before they can even get their pants on." Ash dragged a hand over his face and sighed. "Is all lost? Should we just retreat to the human world?"

Roth glowered at him. "Don't even think of such things. We have fought too hard and too long to keep our home. We will not surrender it to a bunch of self-righteous pricks." Roth spun around and lifted his voice to the sky. "Do you hear me! We are not cowards. We are demons. Do we bow down to angels?"

"No!" The demons stamped their feet in chorus.

"When the Great War was upon us, did we cower in fear and let the traitors take our home?" Roth flapped his wings and hovered above them.

"No!"

"Then why would we now even entertain the idea of letting anyone take our home away? We may be outnumbered, but they are outranked. I have never seen a legion of demons more full of courage, more full of purpose, than those of you standing before me. We will not go quietly into oblivion. If they want us that badly, let's show them what Hell is really made of!"

The demons shouted and called out, shaking the ground with their cheers and stomping feet.

Satisfied that morale had been lifted, Roth landed beside Ash and grabbed him by the shoulders. "Find Lily. I have to set a barrier."

Ash nodded and shifted to leave. Roth stopped him.

"If anything happens...." Roth trailed off, locking eyes with Ash. "You get her out of here, do you understand me?"

Staring back at him, Ash's face hardened as he nodded. "Understood."

Ash transformed into his hellhound form and took off, smoke trailing behind him.

Another alarm sounded, and Roth looked to the east. Dark specks began to form in the sky. At first there were only a few, and then quickly there were too many to count.

It was time.

"Prepare yourselves!" Roth called out as he took his place in front. His wings out wide, Roth lifted his hands and allowed his power to flow through him, pushing it out and expanding it all around them. The air wavered where the shield appeared, the thin barrier of protection wrapping around the palace and all who were in it. Roth had to hope that it would be enough.

Tension thrummed through the air as they all waited for the angels to descend on them. There were so many of them that Roth could feel the morale in his demons sink down to the lowest pits of Hell. There was no way they were going to make it out alive. His eyes shifted over his shoulder to where Ash had disappeared. At least he knew Lily would be taken care of.

He smiled slightly to himself. After all these years of searching, of almost giving up hope to find her, he couldn't have imagined a better woman than the one he had come to know and love. Lily was stubborn and chaotic, yet kind and thoughtful to all of those around her. It was no wonder that they were made for one another. Roth would die happy today just having known her. It was a blessing to have even been able to gaze upon her, let alone taste those supple lips and feel the press of her body against his.

Roth's heart swelled with bitter longing. He wished they had more time. That he would get to watch Lily grow into her full power. To see her swollen with their child. He tried to imagine what their baby would look like. A girl, because who else could pull off that wicked tongue of hers? She would have his ashy blonde hair and Lily's blue eyes. She'd be the most powerful being in all the realms, and no one would stop her.

"Here they come," someone below

called out, jerking Roth out of his daydream.

He braced himself for impact as the angels came at them. They hit against his barrier with swords and spears, none of them powerful enough to use magic the way that the upper-level angels could. It was one of the only small favors Roth expected from today.

Gabriel, the coward, stayed up above the others, not willing to risk his neck in his own war. Roth glared at him and wished he had the power to hold the barrier and knock the preening bird out of the sky. The angels kept coming, smacking against his barrier like a swarm over angry bees. Roth didn't know how much longer he was going to be able to hold it. He could feel his power draining already. If something didn't turn in their favor, then it was all going to be over the moment his shield dropped.

Then they would all be doomed.

Ash

Leaving Roth at the front lines was one of the hardest things Ash had ever had to do. The only thing that compared was when he had to leave Raven's burning apartment behind. Nevertheless, he owed this much to his friend.

He had to find Lily. Ash could at least do that. It wasn't like she could be far. It wasn't like she knew anyone else in Hell.

Servants were gathering valuables and their children, making for the portal on the other side of the palace. While most of the demons in Hell had some kind of abilities, some were less than useless in a battle and were better off escaping to Earth. The children most certainly needed to be evacuated.

"Mama!" a little blue-haired child cried and held all four arms up in the air.

Ash glanced around for its parent but, not seeing anyone claiming the child, stopped at their side. "Hello there, what's your name?"

"Demi," the child sniffed and swiped their nose with their arm. "Have you seen my mama?"

"Well," Ash paused and stretched his neck out, looking once more. "I'm not sure. Do you know what she looks like? Where does she work?"

Having something else to focus on, the child stopped crying and scratched their head. "She is as tall as a mountain, with razor-sharp claws and the best kisses."

Uh... that was helpful.

"How about where she works?" Ash asked. The child just stared up at him. Ash tried again, "Where does she spend her time in the palace?"

"Oh, the kitten." The child pointed back in the other direction.

"Ah," Ash nodded. "She works in the kitchens."

"Yep, yep." The child clapped all four of their hands and smiled up at Ash. "Will you help me find my mama?"

Ash grimaced. He had a duty to carry out and couldn't very well go scouring all over the palace for one child's parent. On the other hand, he couldn't just leave them there. No one else was even paying the lost child any mind.

Sighing, Ash held out his hand. "All right. Let's go."

"Up. Up." The child held his arms out to Ash.

Before Ash could say no, the child climbed him like a monkey, and Ash was the tree. Scowling, Ash walked toward the kitchen, holding tight to the child as they pushed through the crowd. Why was it whenever Ash needed something, there wasn't a servant in sight, and yet when there was an emergency, there were too many of them?

Lily, stay put and safe. I'm coming.

Ash hoped the frustrating woman would stay out of harm's way long enough for him to make his way to her. Knowing his luck, she was already neck-deep in trouble and sinking fast. Ash was just thankful that Raven was safe at home with Michael and not here.

Lily

The black leather pants clung to Lily's butt like a second skin. The top wasn't much better. The top laced up the front and left her shoulders and cleavage bare.

"Are you sure about this?" Lily asked Bacchii, shifting in place. "How is this going to protect me?"

Bacchii rolled her eyes. "Calm yourself, Your Majesty. There is more." She held out a metal and leather piece that wasn't much more than straps and bits.

Lily's brows furrowed. "Where does that go?"

"Here." Bacchii came up behind her and slid one side over Lily's shoulders and then the other side, tying it in place around her chest and then along her arms. Metal plates sat on her shoulders, and the leather lined the bare bits of her arms until it reached her elbows and forearms, which were also covered in the same metal.

Bacchii stepped back, and "There, isn't that better?"

Lily turned this way and that, frowning. "Uh. Sure. What about shoes?" Lily pointed down to her bare feet.

Holding up a finger, signaling for Lily to wait, Bacchii dug into the back of the cabinet where she had found the rest of her clothing. The armory had mostly emptied by the time Bacchii and Lily had made their way there. All of the demons were either leaving the palace or heading to the front line. Lily was anxious to get there as well, but Bacchii wouldn't hear of it without getting her fully outfitted.

"You might have the power, but no one is going to quake in fear of a girl in her night-robe," Bacchii had scoffed at

Lily's clothing before bullying her into letting her dress her up.

"Where will you go?" Lily asked Bacchii as she came out of the closet with a pair of boots with more hooks and laces than Lily knew what to do with.

Bacchii shrugged a shoulder. "This is my home. I will not run like some cockroach does from the light. I will find somewhere to be, and I will fight."

Lily stepped into one of the shoes and then the other, allowing Bacchii to kneel before her and lace them up. "I don't know what will happen next, Bacchii, but I'm glad that I got to meet you."

Smiling up at Lily, Bacchii finished with her shoes. "I am glad to have met you as well, Your Majesty."

"Please," Lily placed her hand on her shoulder. "Call me Lily."

Nodding, Bacchii said, "Lily, then."

Bacchii didn't put any armor on once she was finished with Lily. When Lily asked her about it, Bacchii tapped her skin and winked. "Nothing gets through this unless I want it to."

Lily pushed back the images those words implied and focused on the task at hand. She had to get to the front and help hold the angels back. From the way the others had been talking, she already knew they were sorely undermanned. There just weren't enough demons left in

Hell to take on all the angels Gabriel had brought. They would need some kind of miracle to get out of this alive.

Still, Lily would not run. This was the first place she had felt like herself...ever. She didn't have to hide here. There was no need to put a damper on her power for fear of the others around her. No one here called her a freak. Plus, this was her home. Her mother and father's home. She wouldn't let the angels have it.

"Let's go." Lily nodded to Bacchii and headed out of the armory.

There were still servants scattered around the palace trying to get their families and belongings before they left. The crowd parted for Lily as she came by, sending her looks as if they were expecting her to save them all. She held back a grimace. Lily sure as hell hoped not. While she and Roth had been training every day for the last few years, she was hardly ready to save all seven rings of Hell. If anything, she would be a footnote in this battle. The young heir that was tested too soon before Utopia crushed her.

"You've got this." Bacchii placed a hand on her shoulder, giving it a squeeze. "Remember, your powers only get you so far. It's all about attitude."

Swallowing her fear of failure, Lily straightened her back and forced her eyes forward. A confident smirk slid up her face as she passed by the cheering crowds. That smirk wavered slightly at the sight of Ash waiting, his mouth agape.

"I don't know why I'm surprised." Ash shook his head with a smile. "You always did find a way to be in the middle of all the chaos."

Lily shrugged. "I don't know what you mean." She smacked him on the shoulder and grinned. "Let's go kick some angel ass."

Ash shook his head. "You need to stay back as much as you can. If any angels get through the front lines, we can take them out, but don't go charging into the midst of it."

Lily stepped away from him, frowning. "What are you talking about? I'm not going to just stand aside while the rest of Hell fights for our home. My home."

Grabbing her arm, Ash pulled her to the side, away from prying ears. "Roth wants me to keep you safe, and that's exactly what I'm going to do."

Scoffing, Lily jerked her arm from his grasp. "And what about him? Is he just going to martyr himself like some lamb at the slaughter? I won't have it. I'm the heir. I will not sit idly by while the men protect me," Lily spat out before turning on her heel and marching out of the palace.

None of the history books or war movies prepared Lily for what laid before her. Their little army stood at the ready behind a wavering shield held up by her love, Astaroth. On the other side of that layer of power were hundreds, thousands, more than Lily could ever count filling the sky and ground below. They attacked the protective shield one right after the other, like bugs smacking against a car's windshield. Each hit made Roth's body flinch, and Lily knew he was close to falling. How could he let himself be endangered like that?

"Lily," Ash yelled, grabbing her shoulder. "We need to go. Quickly, before the shield falls."

Lily shook her head. "No. No. I won't go. I won't leave him. Not like this."

"He wouldn't want you to die for him, Lily. Think of your future." Ash tried once more to pull her away, but she dug her heels in.

"He is my future!" Lily shoved some power into her hand, flinging Ash a few feet away. Not enough to hurt him but enough to stun. Rushing forward, Lily scrambled down the stairs, practically jumping them just to get to the bottom. Then she found herself in the back of a sea of demons. How could Lily get to him in time? Oh, what she wouldn't do for wings right about then.

A gasp came over the demons, and Lily's gaze followed theirs. A lone figure flew apart from the others, a ball of light building in their hand. Trying to push through the crowd, tears streamed down Lily's face.

"Roth!" she screamed in a panic, trying to get his attention. "Roth, run. Get out of the way."

He either couldn't hear her or wouldn't go. Either way, it left Lily to watch from the middle of their army, unable to get to the front in time as a beam of light shot out and pierced Roth through the side. His scream of agony was the worst thing she had ever heard in her life, and something she promised herself she would never hear again.

Lily ran back into the palace.

The hallways were mostly deserted. Everyone who lived there was either out in the front fighting or had left for Earth. It made it that much faster to get through the halls and to the set of black double doors.

The crown was whispering to her even before she touched the door. Steeling herself, Lily shoved it open and stalked across the room. This time, her mind stayed her own. Probably because the crown didn't have to persuade her to come closer. To reach out and take it. Lily wanted to take it. She needed it. They all did, or else all was lost.

Her fingers wrapped around the metal of the crown. The first thing that came to Lily's mind was how warm the crown felt. It should have been cold, sitting here in this empty room all alone, and yet it was almost too hot to touch.

The whispers Lily had heard before were louder now that she was holding the crown. They seeped into her ears and shook through her very being. They egged her on, telling her to place the crown on her head. To take the power she needed and she so rightly deserved.

Lily didn't need much encouragement. Right now, Roth was out there hurt, possibly dying. She couldn't let it all go to shit just because she was too afraid to take the power she needed. Lifting the crown, Lily expected it to be hard to put on, that maybe some force would push against her as she placed it on her head. And yet, it was as easy as breathing.

The moment the crown touched Lily's head, she felt whole, complete. As if her entire life, she had been waiting for this moment, and it had finally come. All the power of Hell flowed through her veins, making the magic in her faster, hotter. Lily cried out as a searing pain shot through her back.

Material ripped and heavy white wings sprouted behind her. Lily gasped in pain, glancing behind her to admire the latest addition to her person before righting herself once more.

Lily stared down at her hands, power quickly coming to now, and she wondered how she had ever lived without this feeling. She wasn't just the heir to Hell. She was its queen, and no one was going to take it away from her. No one.

Shoving off the ground, Lily burst through the roof of the palace, not bothering with doors. Why should she? It was her palace. If she wanted to make a new skylight so as to get there faster, then she would. Who would stop her?

The angels were pushing their way through the barrier that Roth had put up. Vaguely she realized that meant that her mate was still alive in the fray somewhere. While she had taken the crown to save him, the only thing on her mind now was keeping the angels out of her kingdom.

Lily soared through the sky, above all the others. Her power poured out of her, shielding each and every member of Hell from the angel scum that thought they could dare attack her home. Her kingdom.

The power in her screamed, *mine,*

mine, mine. It demanded recompense for the audacity, and Lily knew precisely where to get it. Her eyes skimmed the sky until she could find the lone figure high above the rest.

Out of harm's way, most likely. Lily sneered.

Pushing her new wings, Lily made for the leader of them all. Gabriel. She would have his head on a platter and bathe in the blood of his armies for daring to come against the new queen of Hell.

Lucifer

"We're almost there," Raven encouraged him, holding most of his weight against her as they walked through the darkened park.

Lucifer had hoped he would have recovered his strength by the time they reached Hell, and yet that seemed like a farfetched dream now. His injured wing dragged behind him. Pain caused it to throb and twinge. It hurt too much even to put them away. It made him feel sorry for Raven's burden with their extra weight.

"I cannot tell you how grateful I am that you walked into my cell," Lucifer gasped out, wincing with each step they took. The portal to Hell was just a few blocks away, and then he would see his daughter for the first time in centuries. He could make it that far. He would make it that far. Lucifer hadn't come all this way to stop now.

Raven made shushing sounds. "Save your strength. We still have a ways to go."

Lucifer conceded, choosing to let his eyes travel over the world around him. The Earth had changed since the last time he had been on it. The humans had far surpassed his expectations for them. Once they were barely crawling about the Earth, and now they were making metal buildings that reached the sky. They'd even figured out how to fly without wings. He regretted letting himself be locked up for so long. There was so much that he missed.

Raven must have seen the wonder in his eyes because she said, "It's even better than it looks."

"Where are all the humans?"

Pausing at a nearby bench, Raven helped him sit down. "I need a moment. Then we can keep going." She collapsed on the bench beside him, making Lucifer feel worse about the burden he was. "The humans are likely sleeping. At least in this part of the world." She gestured to the greenery around them. "It's a good thing too, because I don't know how I would explain this." Raven waved a hand at his bloodied wings and let out a small laugh.

"No, I suppose we can't traumatize

the poor humans," Lucifer drawled. "They were always so easily spooked."

Shaking her head, Raven said, "Not anymore. Now there are movies and video games. Most of them would likely think we are cosplaying or going to work before they'd believe we're actually real angels."

Lucifer frowned at the foreign words. "Cosplaying?"

Raven leaned her elbows on her knees and explained, "Dressing up. Playing pretend. Usually as characters from books, movies, television shows." Seeing the confusion on his face, Raven sighed. "I'll have to show you sometime. It's too hard to explain right now. Anyway...." She pushed up to her feet. "We should get going. I don't know how much of a head start Gabriel has on us. And I'd like to see my friends before they all die."

"They're not going to die."

Lucifer turned to the familiar voice. "Mike, what are you doing here?"

Michael landed a few feet away from them in full battle regalia, his flaming sword at his side. "Hello, brother." He stepped toward them, his gaze not on Lucifer but Raven. "When you didn't return, I went out to look for you. Then I saw Gabriel's troops moving out. It didn't take much prodding to find out his plans." He made a disgusted sound in the back of his throat. "No soldiers of mine would have given out vital information so easily."

Lucifer nodded. "Things certainly have gone downhill in my absence."

Arching a brow, Michael snorted. "Your absence? What makes you think that you have any sway over our armies?"

Lucifer shifted in his seat, holding back a grimace. "Admit it. When I allowed you to capture me, your armies got lazy. I cut them down like weeds."

Raven chuckled.

"Are you saying you agree with him?" Michael asked his daughter.

Shrugging, Raven shifted her weight from one leg to the other. "I know what I saw, and I think Lucifer is right. Now, if you're done arguing like an old married couple, we have places to be, people to save."

Raven reached for him, and Lucifer allowed her to help him to his feet.

"What's wrong with you?" Michael asked, coming to help Lucifer stand. "You let someone hurt you?"

Lucifer grunted in response.

"And here you were talking down to our armies," Michael chuckled, "Are you rusty, brother?"

"Hey, he fought off hundreds of angels to get us here, and that asshole

Raphael. Don't criticize unless you can say the same."

Michael's brows shot to his hairline. "You must have done quite a bit to gain my daughter's approval. She is not easily won over."

Lucifer noticed the tension between the two of them. "I can imagine. I will admit I am not sure about my own reunion with my daughter. What if she doesn't want anything to do with me?"

Raven hugged his side as they began to make the painstaking trek to the portal. "Just give her a chance. Lily hasn't had the best of lives. I think she wants you as much as you want her."

Her words made Lucifer's heart swell with hope. Hope that he would see his daughter once more and have the relationship with her that he had always dreamed of before those in Utopia had taken it away from him.

They made it to the swirling portal without much of a problem, though there was a human walking their small creature at one point. The human took one look at them, frowned before shaking their head, and walked on their way. Perhaps Raven was right. Humans weren't even fazed by what they saw anymore. It made Lucifer wonder what it would take to make the humans cower like they did of old.

"Here we are," Raven announced, stopping before the portal. "Are you ready?"

Lucifer stared at the portal. This was it. He would finally get to meet his daughter again. He hadn't been this nervous since the first time he had spoken to her mother, Lilith. In fact, he might be more anxious now than he had been then.

"You'll do fine," Raven reassured him, offering him a smile. "Let's just all survive the day, and then you can worry about everything else later."

Inclining his head, Lucifer silently agreed. His anxiety about meeting his daughter could wait. There were more pressing problems. Leagues of them, just waiting to kill them all.

"Well, there is no time like the present." Michael pushed them forward and through the portal.

Thankfully, this portal brought them to just outside the center of Hell. Lucifer didn't think he'd be able to make the perilous journey across all seven rings. Not today. He wanted to see what had become of his kingdom in his absence, but it would have to wait.

"Shit," Raven hissed. "We're too late."

Lucifer pulled away from her and Michael's grasp and stumbled forward. Thousands and thousands of angels filled the field between where they stood and the palace, with Gabriel at their head.

It was easy to see the number of demons protecting the palace was paltry in comparison. They were going to be destroyed entirely, and there was nothing he could do about it.

"What do we do?" Raven cried out. "How do we defeat all of this?"

Michael unsheathed his flaming sword, his gaze hard. "We go for the head. Kill Gabriel, and the rest will flounder. They are nothing without their leader."

"He's right," Lucifer explained. "If Gabriel falls, they will turn to the next archangel available, and Michael can stop them."

"They wouldn't listen to you?" Raven inquired.

Michael and Lucifer exchanged a look before throwing their heads back and laughing.

"No," Lucifer stated through pants of painful laughter. "Most wouldn't even remember who I am, let alone follow me if they knew."

"So, what are we waiting for?" Raven stepped toward the fray. Lucifer stopped her with a hand.

He felt it.

The pull on his heart. The one thing that had kept him from keeping his mate and daughter safe. It was coming to him. No, wait. It belonged to someone else now.

Lucifer pushed back the pain and shot into the sky. He zipped over the angels below, most of them not seeing him until he had long passed by. He reached the front of the line just below the palace steps.

"Lucifer!" Gabriel called out. "How nice of you to join us. Are you here to see me destroy your kingdom and your heir in one fell swoop?"

Ignoring the archangel, Lucifer stared in the direction of the pull. A moment later, Lilith stood before him. No, not Lilith. His daughter. Lily. White wings spread out behind her, and her violet hair flowed in the air as if some invisible wind came from her. Then he saw it. There, sitting on the top of her head, power radiating from it, was the Wicked Crown.

Her blue eyes, so much like his own, settled on him, and Lucifer grinned wickedly.

His daughter, his *heir*.

She had finally returned, and she was glorious.

The End

About the Authors

Erin Bedford is an otaku, recovering coffee addict, and Legend of Zelda fanatic. Her brain is so full of stories that need to be told that she must get them out or explode into a million screaming chibis. Obsessed with fairy tales and bad boys, she hasn't found a story she can't twist to match her deviant mind full of innuendos, snarky humor, and dream guys.

On the outside, she's a work from home mom and bookbinger. On the inside, she's a thirteen-year-old boy screaming to get out and tell you the pervy joke they found online. As an ex-computer programmer, she dreams of one day combining her love for writing and college credits to make the ultimate video game!

Until then, when she's not writing, Erin is devouring as many books as possible on her quest to have the biggest book gut of all time. She's written over thirty books, ranging from paranormal romance, urban fantasy, and even sci-fi romance.

Follow her on social media:
Website | Facebook | Twitter | Instagram | Newsletter | Facebook Group

May Sage is a geek, who much prefers getting lost in fictional world than dealing with reality. She's been writing since she was eight. As a little girl, everyone told her becoming an author was practically impossible, but she's a Capricorn, so she turned around and said "watch me."

She has various fur babies—a German Shepherd, two savannahs, and an adorable something-or-other with puppy dog eyes.

Her greatest aspiration is writing characters that make people want to throw their books at walls and wail in despair, or laugh hard enough to consider reading as an abs workout.

You can stalk her at: Facebook | Instagram | Website | Newsletter | May Sage's Coven on Facebook for news, giveaways, and fun stuff <3

www.ingramcontent.com/pod-product-compliance
Lightning Source LLC
Chambersburg PA
CBHW061301210726

48293CB00003B/1068